You Know

Dat Boudreaux Ain't Me,

It's Ma Cousin.

By Larry Boudreaux

Cover illustration by Eric J. Cantrelle

1st Printing 1999
2nd Printing 1999
3rd Printing 2000
4th Printing 2002
5th Printing 2005
6th Printing 2007

Published by
Boudreaux Cajun General Store
P.O. Box 87163
Baton Rouge, LA 70879

ISBN: 0-9676002-0-0

Printed in the United States of America
Moran Printing
Baton Rouge, LA

Dedications and Acknowledgements

This book is dedicated to my Lord Jesus, who has given me so many undeserved blessings.

To my late wife, Rosemary, who demonstrated patience and put up with me working on the computer all hours of the night.

To all of my friends who shared Boudreaux stories; thereby, giving me the basic idea for this book.

To my children, Michelle and Michael, who were excited and supportive when they heard dad was writing a book of Boudreaux stories.

I'd like to extend a special thanks to Alon Willett, who helped me proofread this book and allowed me to keep my day job while working on the project.

I'd like to extend a special thanks to Tony Boudreau (He's not my cousin) for the help he extended to me with his constructive criticism and technical advice regarding this book.

About the Author

Larry Boudreaux lives in Baton Rouge, Louisiana. He is a direct tenth generation descendant of Michel Boudrot and Michelle Aucoin who were born in France and settled in Acadia. (originally Nova Scotia where all Cajuns (Acadians) started.)

Later his ancestors settled in and around the Bayou LaFouche area located in what is today Assumption Parish, Louisiana.

His grandfather was a blacksmith on a sugar plantation in Iberville Parish before deciding to move his large family to Baton Rouge for it's opportunities.

Larry was born in New Orleans, LA during WWII, where his dad served in the US Merchant Marines.

Larry was raised in Baton Rouge, graduated from Baton Rouge High, and served in the US Navy for four years.

He is a Viet-Nam Veteran. After attending two years at LSU, he moved to Houston, TX to join the working world as a sales trainee for a major office machine manufacturer. He was transferred to Tennessee as sales manager, where he also finished his BS in Business at the University of Tennessee. He transferred back to Houston where he became a partner in successful business.

Larry always missed his Louisiana roots and came back home in 1990.

He says there is no place like home, especially if it is in Louisiana. He is very proud of his heritage and wants to do what he can to make others understand the logic of this unique place.

He knows that a lot of people who don't live in Louisiana feel that Cajuns are just a bunch of backward people.

Larry asks, "What standard determines backward?

Could it be, enjoying life with God, your family, and your friends?"

Just remember that Louisiana is a full functioning state. We don't have to import our doctors, lawyers, engineers, etc. We grow our own. In fact we do it with a sense of humor.

Table of Contents

The best way to enjoy this book

There are several ways for you to get the most enjoyment out of this book.

Initially part of the fun you can expect from this book, is trying to read the Cajun dialect.

You may have to read some of these stories several times before you will be able to adapt a natural Cajun story telling flow for your personality.

It can be a lot of fun to practice and become a Cajun storyteller. Study the short dictionary. Be aware of the Cajun culture. Share these stories with your friends

You can use this book as a reference by going back to it from time to time.

You can have the perfect Cajun party for your friends. Invite your friends over for a Cajun meal from this book, play some Cajun music, and share some of the stories about my cousin Boudreaux.

You can have a lot of fun with this book. It may require a little work on your part. In the long run you will be amused.

If you are busy, like a lot of us these days, I will have an audio tape available soon with my favorite stories on it. It will be entertaining as well as helpful.

Contact me using the information in the back of this book. I will let you know as soon as the tapes are ready to be shipped.

Plan a Cajun party?

and

Invite ma cousin Boudreaux

Laisez le bon temps rouller.

If you don't know what I am referring to. Read the previous page of this book, in the section. ***The best way to enjoy this book.***

SOME WORDS YOU NEED TO KNOW

A Few Words/Phrases
That Will Help You Understand This Book Better.

adieu: (*ah-do*) goodbye

Atchafalaya: (*a-cha-fa-lie-ya*) a swamp basin and river in south Louisiana.

ax: (*axe*) the process of questioning, ask. "Ax you momma kang you go."

bayou: (*bah-yoo*) small river

beignets: (*ben-yays*) French donuts

boudin: (*boo-dan*) A sausage made with rice and meat stuffing such as pork, beef, crawfish, shrimp, etc. Originally made with pork and the blood of the hog. (boudin rouge)

bourre: (*boo-ray*) Cajun card game in which the loser of the hand must "Stuff" or match the take of the winning hand

Cajun: (*Ca-jun*) an abbreviation for the word "Acadian", a person from the area of Nova Scotia, Canada called Acadia.

cafe au lait: (*kah-fay-oh-lay*) coffee with milk

chalon: (*sha-lon*) moving boat store which traveled along the bayous.

cher: (*share*) an endearing term can be used instead of dear

cochon de lait: (*koh-shon-duh-lay*) "suckling pig", a pig roast

couche couche: (*koosh-koosh*) a Cajun cornmeal cereal, usually eaten with milk or syrup

crawfish: (*craw-fish*) a crustacean that is harvested by the Cajuns for food, also known as a mud bug.

Creole: (*cre-ole)* translated, "creole" means "native". In South Louisiana it refers to the combination of French and Spanish cultures with African and Indian influences.

de: (*de*) "the"

dem: (*dem*) "them"

dere: (*dare*) "there"

do-do: (*doh-doh*) A short form of the french word "dormier" (to sleep).

etouffee: (*ay-too-fay*) "smothered in its own juice", the ultimate Cajun dish, usually made with seafood in a smothered vegetable sauce

fais-do-do: (*fay-doh-doh*) country-dance, where the children are brought and they sleep.

garcon: (*gar-son*) Cajun youth, male, waiter.

gratis: (*gra-shus*) free.

guarontee: (*gua-ron-tee*) "guarantee, or to be positively sure."

gumbo: (*gum-boh*) a roux-based soup of poultry, sausage, or seafood, served over rice

jamais de la vie: (*jwah-may day lie-vee*) oh, but never.

jambalaya: (*jam-buh-ly-uh)* a rice dish made with meats and vegetables

joie de vivre: (*jwah-duh-vee*) "love of life"

joli: (*jwoh-lee*) pretty, cute

laisez le bon temps rouller: (*les (e)le-baw(n)-taw(n)-roll(e)*) "let the good times roll"

lagniappe: (*lan-yappe*) A little extra. Usually when someone gives a little more than is expected.

le bon Dieu: (*lay-Bo(n) Day(e)*) the good God.

ma chere: (*ma-shar-(e*)) my dear.

mais: (*may*) but.

mais oui: (*may wee*) but yes

mais non: (*may non*) but no

Mardi Gras: (*mar-dee-graw*) "Fat Tuesday", a day of celebration on the last Tuesday before Lent

marchand: (*mar-shan*) merchant, shopkeeper, also a surname.

mieux: (*mew*) better, more.

nutria: (*nu-tra*) a large rodent like animal found in south Louisiana that provides excellent fur and food.

oui: (*wee)* yes.

passer: un bon temps: (*pah-say-un-baw(n)-taw(n)*) "have a good time" or pass a good time

petit: (*pa-teet*) very small.

pecan: (*pih kawn*) not pee-kan

pirogue: (*pee-row*) small boats used by the Cajuns on the bayou

poupon: (*poo pon*) baby, infant

pralines: (*praw-leens*) candy made from pecans, brown sugar, and cream.

rat cheer: (*rat-cheer*) right here, in front of you.

sac-a'-lait: (*sack-a lay*) freshwater fish, crappe

tasso: (*tas-sew*) Cajun jerky which is hotly seasoned for use in cooking vegetables.

tata: (*ta-ta*) thank you to Cajun bebe.

t'ing: (*ting*) "thing

ti: (*tee*) small, petite, or little.

traylor: (*tra-lor*) "trailer"

vieux: (*vuu*) old.

visite: (*vee-zeet*) visit

wit': (*wit*) "with"

zydeco: (*zah-dee-koh*) "les haricots" meaning "snap beans", Its a nickname for the unique Creole Music that features a large accordion

---

Everybody Enjoys a Good Cajun Story

Everyone has a book inside him or her. Some people have an exciting autobiography, while others can write a fictional story. I have been blessed with the name Boudreaux.

The Boudreaux name is very common in South Louisiana. Almost all Boudreaux's can be traced back to one ancestor, Michel Boudrot from Nova Scotia. He had eleven children and most of his heirs were very prolific having as many as nineteen children. Today there are over 10, 000 Boudreaux descendants.

To give you an idea, several years ago, I went to visit the mayor of Thibodaux, Louisiana. I didn't have an appointment. His secretary told me the mayor was in a budget meeting and it was lasting longer than expected.

As I was telling her that I would return later, the mayor came through the door. She announced that Larry Boudreaux was here to see him, and he invited me in.

Once in his office, he looked at me in a puzzled manner and said, "I know two Larry Boudreaux's, and you are neither one of them."

He nonetheless invited me in for a cup of coffee and visit. Even though he was tired from his budget meeting and had never met me before, I had to excuse myself an hour later to leave for my next appointment.

This is the way the Cajun people are. They are somewhat clannish before they get to know you. Then they are very hospitable and friendly. (The Boudreaux name was familiar to the mayor; therefore, he felt that he knew me.)

In South Louisiana whenever someone tells a Cajun story or joke, the main Character is more often than not named Boudreaux. Usually Boudreaux has wife named Marie and a dog named Phideaux. Boudreaux has a friend named Thibodeaux who has a wife named Clotile. These Cajun stories have been floating around the bayous for a long time.

Practically every time I introduce my self as Larry Boudreaux, the person I'm speaking with inevitably has to share me their latest Boudreaux story. I personally think these stories are funny and enjoy sharing them.

About ten years ago, I was at a Police Jury convention in Baton Rouge. (Louisiana Police Jurors hold a position that is equivalent to a County Commissioner in other states).

On the last day of the convention, a state representative, who was running for governor, was working the convention floor with his entourage. When I introduced myself as Larry Boudreaux he got excited and said "Oh Boudreaux, Dat's de name I use when I check into hotels."

Usually the Boudreaux character in Cajun stories is supposed to be stereotypical of the funny side of the Cajun culture.

Boudreaux is a Cajun man who works hard every day. He loves his God, his family and having fun with his friends. He definitely lives to "laisez le bon temps rouller" (let the good times roll.)

Lots of Boudreaux stories could be Polish jokes in Chicago or Aggie jokes in Texas. What gives these stories their special flavor is our Cajun culture.

Cajuns are different. They tend have an unconventional view as to what most people believe to be traditional. You can see the differences in their food, their politics, and their lifestyles. Cajuns want to be left alone to live their lives without outside interference.

You can see why Cajuns act the way they do once you look at their Acadian history which started in Canada when the Anglo-Protestant King of England tried to force the Franco-Catholic Acadians of Nova Scotia to swear their allegiance to him and the Church of England.

They did not consider themselves English or French. They were now Acadians in the New World. They refused to swear their allegiance and as a result, were exiled for their beliefs.

Some of the Acadians went to south Louisiana. Most lived in the Swamps where they could be independent of politics, raise their family, praise their God.

Most Cajuns (a shortened version of de word Acadians) chose to work hard by hunting, fishing, trapping.

When I hear someone telling a Boudreaux joke or when

I am sharing these stories about Boudreaux with friends, I always tell them, "let there be no mistake, this story is not about me, but it's my cousin Boudreaux." That one statement is the basis for the title of this book.

I now want to share with you these Boudreaux stories which highlight some of the good parts of the state where I live and people I love. Hopefully, when you finish this book, you will feel the same way.

There is a lot of information available regarding the Cajun people and their culture. If you try to study this heritage, you will find it is very rich and runs deep.

The people of south Louisiana are proud of their culture. There are cultural exhibits all over the state in museums and historical sites. Visitors are always welcome to come and share these with us.

For those who would like to dig deeper into Acadian history, there are numerous research sources in the libraries and on the Internet.

Suggested Books on Louisiana Acadian History

The founding of New Acadia : the beginnings of Acadian life in Louisiana, *1765-1803* / by Carl A. Brasseaux.

A selected bibliography of Acadian history, culture, & genealogy 1955-1985 / by Carl A. Brasseaux.

Quest for the promised land: official correspondence relating to the first Acadian migration to Louisiana, 1764-1769 / translated by Carl A. Brasseaux, Emilio Fabian Garcia, and Jacqueline K. Voorhies; edited by Carl A. Brasseaux ; annotated by Carl A. Brasseaux

Acadian-Cajun genealogy step-by-step / by Timothy Hebert.

Acadian-Cajun genealogical periodical article index / compiled by Timothy R. Hebert

Youth in Acadie: reflections on Acadian life and culture in southwest Louisiana / by George Arceneaux.

Just look a little and you will find that there are plenty of books regarding the Cajun culture in the library.

A couple of suggested websites to research Cajun History and Genealogy.

http://www.acadian-cajun.com
http://www.genforum.com

There are several links that will give you more information about Louisiana and it's Cajun culture.

Visit my Website.
http://Cousin.Boudreaux.com

Have fun.

Laisez le bon temps rouller

You know Dat Boudreaux Ain't Me, It's Ma Cousin

1. Boudreaux bought a thermos bottle.

Boudreaux went to The Wal-Mart store. He saw a sign advertising thermos bottles on sale. He asked the clerk "watt's a termos bottle?" (Since he had never seen one before). The clerk told him that it was something to keep hot things hot and cold things cold. Boudreaux said, "dat sounds great", and bought one.

A short time later his friend Thibodeaux saw him and asked what was he carrying under his arm. Boudreaux said: "Oh, dis is a termos bottle." Thibodeaux asked: "What does eet do?" Boudreaux said: "Eet keeps hot t'ings hot and cold t'ings cold." Thibodeaux said "dat sounds good, what do you have in eet now?"

Boudreaux's said, "Well, rat now, I have tree Popsicle's and two cups of coffee in eet."

2. Boudreaux showed off Phideaux to hees frien' Thibodeaux.

Boudreaux and Thibodeaux were very competitive when it came to their duck hunting dogs.

Boudreaux bought a new dog, named it Phideaux, and started to train it.

When Phideaux was ready, Boudreaux took him to the duck blind for a test. After a little while some ducks flew over and Boudreaux shot one (BANG). Phideaux took off at Boudreaux's signal, walked on top of the water to retrieve the duck, and he then walked back.

Boudreaux looked in disbelief. Then some more ducks flew over, and Boudreaux shot two of them (BANG-BANG). Sure enough, Phideaux retrieved both of them by walking on top of the water.

At this point Boudreaux was really confused and thought to himself, "When I tell Thibodeaux, he will t'ink I'm crazy. I don't want to tell him and let him t'ink I'm crazy, I'll have to invite him out here and let him see for himself."

A few days later, Boudreaux and his friend Thibodeaux went with their dogs to the duck blind. Some ducks flew over (BANG). One duck was hit. Phideaux walked on the water and retrieved the duck. Boudreaux looked at Thibodeaux, who showed no expression on his face.

Some more ducks flew over. (BANG...BANG). Two ducks were down. Again, Phideaux walked on the water to retrieve de ducks. Thibodeaux still showed no reaction.

Boudreaux couldn't stand it anymore. He asked Thibodeaux, "Have you noticed anything strange 'bout Phideaux?" Thibodeaux replied, "Why I sure did, dat dang' dog can't swim."

3. Boudreaux an' Thibodeaux were bot' qualified de same for da job.

Boudreaux and Thibodeaux were looking for a job. They went to the same company to apply for the same job, took the same exam, and interviewed with the same manager.

The manager informed them that they had both scored the same on the exam and were equally qualified, but that only one could be hired. He'd have to come up with a way to determine which one he would hire.

His solution was to ask both two questions, and to hire the one with the best answers.

He started by asking Thibodeaux, "What are the two days of the week that start with T?" Thibodeaux answered, "Well lets see, dar's Tuesday and T'ursday."

The manager then asked, "How many seconds are in a year?" Thibodeaux stood quietly, looking at the ceiling and walls, and then said, "Oh, I can't figure dat out wit'out ma calculator!"

He then asked Boudreaux, "What are the two days of the week that start with T." Boudreaux quickly answered, "Oh dat's easy eet's today and tomorrow."

The manager then asked, "How many seconds are in a year?" Boudreaux replied, "Twelve."

Curious about this answer thee manager asked, "How do you figure only 12 seconds in a year?"

Boudreaux replied, “Jus t’ink bout eet. Dere is January de 2nd, February de 2nd, March...”

4. Leettle Pierre Boudreaux tells about Davie Crockett.

One day at the schoolhouse, the teacher, during the history class, asked Little Pierre Boudreaux to tell something about Davie Crockett.

Little Pierre piped up and said, “Davie Crockett killed a Cajun.”

The teacher asked, “What do you mean?”

Leettle Boudreaux said, "look rat chair, de book says he killed Hebert (Pronounced A-bear) when he was only tree.”

5. Boudreaux meets de devil.

One day, Boudreaux died and went to hell. When he got there he sat up on a big rock and just smiled. Later that day the devil walks by, sees Boudreaux smiling, and stops.

Now dat old devil can’t stand to see anyone happy down dare wit’ him, so he axed Boudreaux, “Why are you smiling?”

Boudreaux says, “Because I’m surprised to see dat eet feels like a nice June day in south Louisiana here.”

Well, dat old devil was so mad dat he goes over to termostat and cranked it up to about 50% power.

'Bout an hour later (after de temperature had risen) de devil comes back and sees Boudreaux still sitting on dat rock still smiling. So de Devil asks again, "Why are you still smiling?"

Boudreaux has de same answer, "Because eet is STILL not as hot here as South Louisiana on a good July day!"

Dat devil got so mad dat he goes over to de termostat and cranked eet up to full power.

Well, de same thing happens. De devil walked bye and axed, "Boudreaux, Why are you still smiling?"

Boudreaux says, "Well, eet getting warmer, but eet is just like a day in August in South Louisiana!"

Dat devil ran over to de termostat and kicked eet so hard dat he blew up de whole unit.

Well, bout two hour's later hell is frozen over. De devil walks by dat rock and sees Boudreaux sitting dere shivering wit' a huge grin. De devil is so amazed dat he asks one more time, "Boudreaux, eet is freezing in here, why are you still smiling?"

Boudreaux looks de devil in de eyes and says, "I guess de Saints finally won de Superbowl!"

6. Clement and Boudreaux went huntin' togeder.

Ever since Clement and Boudreaux were young, they hunted and trapped together.

Year after year they would always go out together, split up, and go to their ponds which were right next door to each other. They would meet again after the day's hunt was over.

Boudreaux got married one day an' he stop going along wit' Clement. Rat after dat, he started bringing in tree or fore time as much duck and nutria as Clement. No matter what happen, Boudreaux done got hees limit on whatever was in season, plus a few t'ing de game warden don't want to know bout.

One day, Clement come back wit'out nuttin. He see Boudreaux comin' back home from hunting, an' he decide he gone axe Boudreaux what hees secret was.

He axe Boudreaux, How come eet is dat you always got so much when you brought youself hunting, when we trap an' hunt in de same dam' water, an' me I don't got but a leettle bit?

Boudreaux tole' Clement, "You know my wife?" Clement say, "Ya, Boudreaux, you know I know her; I was you bes' man!"

Boudreaux say, "Clement, you know how ugly she is, huh?"

Clement say, "Boudreaux you know I know dat; I was you bes' man!"

Boudreaux say, Well, Clement, eet's like dis. I brought Mess out to de duck blind wit' me, dere, an' I put a big burlap bag over her head.

Den, when everyt`ing gots real quiet, dere, an` when all de duck and nutria come nosin` aroun`, I jus` whip dat bag off of Mess` head, an` she jus` uglies everyt`ing to death."

"Boudreaux", Clement say, "Mais how come you don't brought you moder-in-law wit' you instead? She 'bout twice as ugly as Mess."

Boudreaux tole Clement, "I tried dat, Clement, but she bust up de ducks too bad!"

7. Boudreaux wants to change hees name.

Boudreaux went to de courthouse to spoke to de judge `bout changing his name.

De judge axed him, "what can de court do for you, sir?"

Boudreaux said, "I'd like to change my name yo honor."

De judge axed him, "Why do you want to change your name?"

Boudreaux replied, "People have been teasing me all of my life cause of my name, and I`m ready to change eet now."

De judge axed, "Well den, what is your name?"

He said, "Poo Poo Boudreaux."

De judge remarked, "I don`t blame you one bit for wanting to change dat name. What do you want to change eet to?"

Boudreaux said, "Poo Poo Fontenot."

8. Boudreaux meets a fast woman from de big city.

When Boudreaux was a young man an' was 'bout to left home to go to de big city for de first time, hees ma-ma call him an' say she had to talk to him 'bout fast women.

Boudreaux left rat after dey talked, an' he deedn' see hees ma-ma until he come back 'bout a month later.

As soon as Boudreaux come back, hees ma-ma take him aside an' axe him, "Son, did you saw any of dem fast women what live in de big city?"

Boudreaux tole hees ma-ma, "Mais, Ma-Ma, de second day I was dere I met one of de fastest women in de 'hole worl! Poo yi, she was some fast!"

Mama Boudreaux tole him, she wanted to hear all bout dat, so he say, "Well, I was walking down de street dere in de big city, an' dere was dis woman what was sittin' on her front porch. She say to me, My mama an' papa ain't home rat now, so eef you want to, you can come in an' have some cookies."

Boudreaux den said. "Well, I went in dere wit' her, an' almost rat away, she start to turn de lights down way low, an' makin' all kind of sweet eyes at me.

I axe her 'bout de cookies, an' she pick up dis tray wit' bout t'ree dozen cookies on eet. She kind of hold dat under her chin, an' say, 'Boo, what you t'ink gone taste sweeter, dese cookies or my lips?'

Rat den an' dere, I just knew she was one of dem fast women you warn me 'bout, Ma-Ma."

Mama Boudreaux axe him, "Ti-Boudreaux, how you knew dat?" Boo say, "Cause, As soon as I grabbed 'bout a half dozen of dem cookies, she took after me wit' a skillet, an' eet took me dang near 2 miles to outrun her!"

9. Boudreaux is standing in his field.

LeBlanc and Trahan were driving down de road pas Boudreaux's house one morning and saw Boudreaux out in hees field.

De next morning, when dey passed by, Boudreaux was still standing out in hees field.

Trahan tole LeBlanc, "Eef Boudreaux is still out dere tomorrow, LeBlanc, let's find out what he is doing." Sure enough, de next morning, Boudreaux was standing in hees field again.

Trahan axed him, "What are you doing out here, Boudreaux?"

He said, "I'm trying to win de Nobel Peace prize." Trahan axed, "What do you mean? How are you gonna win de Nobel Peace prize out here?"

Boudreaux said, "To win, you have to be outstand'n in your field."

10. Rodrique bot a beauteeful parrot from sot' America

Rodrique went to Sot' America to work in dem oilfield, dere. De first t'ing what Rodrique seen when he got dere was dem beauteeful parrot-birds what fly wild all 'round down dere. He say to himself, "Rodrique; you gots to send one of dem bird to you mama back home in Eunice."

So Rodrique, he foun' one of dem bird-train peoples dere what had de most beautimous of all dem birds what Rodrique had done seen. An' talk! Man, cher, dat bird had a bigger vocrabbilary dan Rodrique did, an' could talk in tirteen deefferent languages.

Rodrique bought dat bird for two tousand dollar, and ship dat bird back home to hees mama.

'bout 2 month go by, an' Rodrique, him, he go back home to Eunice. He just can't wait to see hees mama and find out how she liked de bird.

As soon as he walk tru de door, Rodrique axe hees mama, "Ma-ma, how you like dat bird what I sent you?"

Mama Rodrique look at him an' say, "Mais, it was delicious!!!! Made de bes' gumbo what I ever taste!!!"

Rodrique can't believe dat hees Mama had cooked dat spensive parrot-bird. He say, "Mais, Ma-ma, deedn' you know dat bird could talk in 13 deefferent languages and cost me two tousand dollar?"

She look at Rodrique an` tole him, "Eef he was dat darn' smart, how come he deedn` say nothin` an` just squawk like any udder chicken when I grab him an` wrung hees neck to make de gumbo?"

11. Boudreaux and Thibodeaux were proud cause it only took 21 day.

Boudreaux and Thibodeaux were sitting quietly in a bar drinking beer.

In a few minutes dey both shouted, "Only 21 days."

Again, dey shouted, "Eet took only 21 days."

A leettle later dey hollowed out loud, "I can't believe it only took 21 days."

De bartender, who was getting very curious axed, "What took only 21 days?"

Dey said, "Dis 28 piece puzzle here, only took us 21 days to put togeder."

De bartender looked at dem and said, "Dat doesn't look so hard, why are you bragging on something like dat?"

Thibodeaux said, "Look at de box. Eet is suppose` to take 2 to 3 years.

12. Rodrique got heemself anoder parrot.

Rodrique decide he gonna get him anoder parrot-bird.

He go to de pet store an' fine one not quite so pretty or 'spensive as de lass one, an' brought dat home.

After 'bout a month, ti-Rodrique notice dat de parrot-bird done loss all kind of weight. He call de Beterarian an' axe him 'bout what to do.

De bet axe Rodrique to look at de bird's beak an' see eef de top of de beak done growed down over de bottom of de beak where eet wouldn't open.

Rodrigue say, "Mais, jamais, dass juss what happened!" So, de bet tole Rodrique to got a leettle file an' file off juss de end of de parrot-bird's beak so dat de bird could open hees mouth an' eat.

'bout 2 week later, de bet see Rodrique in de store an' axe him, "How dat bird is, Rodrique?"

Rodrique tole him, "De bird's dead, Doc."

De bet axe him, "He died juss from filing off de end of hees beak"

Rodrique say, "Non, Doc, I t'ink he was dead when I uncrank hees head out of de vise after I file down hees beak."

13. Boudreaux sees a tree legged chicken.

Boudreaux was driving hees car down de road when he saw a tree-legged chicken running along side of him. He sped up to 50 mph and de chicken was still running along side of him.

He den pushed de car to 60 mph and de chicken was keeping up wit' him, stride for stride.

At 70 mph, de chicken ran pas him out to a yard.

Boudreaux saw dat dere were lots of chickens, and dey all had tree legs. He could not believe hees own eyes; he stopped and axed de farmer why did he have all dose tree legged chickens.

De farmer tole him dat he had tree children and dey all liked de drumstick. Dats why he raised dose tree-legged chickens.

Boudreaux axed, "how do dey taste."

De farmer tole him, "No one knows, we ain't been able to catch one yet."

14. Clement wants to know why de pig only has tree legs.

Clement went to Boudreaux's house one time to caught up on old times. When Clement had been dere two or tree hour, he saw dis pig what was walk all around de house. Eet only had 3 legs. De pig ack like he owns de place, going all over de inside of de house.

Clement axe Boudreaux, "Man, cher, you out you mind, you? Mais, how come you got dat tree-legged pig what run all around you house like dat for, aah?"

Boudreaux tole Clement, "Dat ain't jus' any pig, Clement, dat's a lifesavin' pig!

Bout a month ago, dat pig jomp in de bayou; pull my wife, Tante, out when she was bout to drown!

An' two week ago, dat pig threw himself in front of a tractor what was bout to roll back over me stopped eet."

Clement say, "Mais, dat muss be how de pig loss hees leg?"

Boudreaux say "No, Clement; a pig dis good, you don't eat dat all at one time, you know."

15. Boudreaux an' Thibodeaux didn't pay any attention to Tante Key at de nursing home.

Tante Key moved into de nursing' home where Boudreaux an' Placid was.

Tante Key was an elderly lady, but taught she still was nice to look at.

So, de first mornin' she move dere, Tante put on a nice dress an' walk out front of de nursin' home where Placide an' Boudreaux was doin' what dey did every day; sittin' on de bench out front an' watchin' all de peoples pass by.

Tante walk up an' down, up an' down, up an' down, rat in front of Placide an' Boudreaux for bout ten minute Dey don't say nonesomeatall to her. She got a leettle put out of herself, dere, an' went inside.

De next mornin', Tante put on a leettle shorter dress, wit' some high heels, gave herself de big hair, an' walk out front again. De same t'ing as she done before.

Boudreaux an` Placide don`t say a t`ing to her.

Dis goes on for quite some time, every day a leettle shorter skirt, a leettle more makeup, an` a leettle higher heels. Nothing worked.

Finally, Tante got so upset, she went in an` put on one of dem leettle string bikini bathing suit an` walk rat in front of Boudreaux an` Placide an` jus` stand dere for bout 5 minutes. Neider one of dem say a t`ing to her, so she get REAL put out of herself, an` go back inside.

'bout 10 minutes later, Boudreaux look at Placide an' say, "Placide, you see what Tante Cey had on dis morning?" Placide say, "Mais, yeah, Boudreaux, an' for Christmas, I`m gonna buy her a steam iron."

16. Thibodeaux decides to learn how to pairashoot.

For long on tree week, Thibodeaux, him, he go to de pairashoot school whatfor to learn himself how to done dat.

De day of de big jomp come. Thibodeaux got heemself in de airplane wit` dat big knapsack full of bedsheet.

Den, when he got high, high up in de sky, Thibodeaux jomp out dat plane an' count to four. (Two of de tree week Thibodeaux spent in dat jomping-out school was on how to get to dat number all de way from one. I`ll guarontee)

Dem big bedsheet come out dat knapsack. Thibodeaux he notice dat dey don`t got none of dem string what supposed to hole dat bedsheet to him.

He fall, and fall, and fall until he get bout two or tree hundred feet from de ground, and he see Boudreaux, flyin' up into de sky, an' he pass Thibodeaux doin' bout a hundred mile an hour.

Thibodeaux axe Boudreaux. "Boudreaux, You know somet'ing 'bout dem pairashoot?" Boudreaux fly pass Thibodeaux an' say, "Mais, non Thibodeaux; You know somet'ing 'bout butane stoves?"

17. Placide bot a hang glider in California.

Placide (pronounced Plah-seed) took heemself on a trip to California. When he got dere, de firs' t'ing he saw was dem handgun-around gliders, wit' dem peoples jomping all off of de mountain what dey got dere. Den dey glide-glide-glide till dey WHOOSH... lan' rat on de groun'.

He watch dat for all day, dere, an' he deedn' even finish hees vacate. He cash in all hees Cajun Axprass travelin' chek what he brought wit' him, an' went an bought one of dem handgun-around gliders for himself.

Den Placide, he brought himself back home to Baton Rouge an' wait on de t'ing to show up in de mail.

Bout tree week later, here come Placide's mailman haulin' Placide's handgun-aroun' glider, all pack up in pieces in a big box.

Placide spent bout tree more week trying' to unfold de instruction, den jus' give up. He got hees crasson-rinch out an' start to put all dem pieces togeder.

When he got dat altogeder, Placide look all over for a mountain to jomp off wit' hees handgun-aroun' glider, but dey don't got too many of dem in Sot Louisiana, I'll guarontee. So Placide, him, he set hees eye on de state capitol building dere in Baton Rouge.

Placide, him, he took dat glider over to de capitol building an' jomp rat off de top. He almost crash de groun' 2 or tree times, before he got da hang of eet, den he start fly all over de place.

He finally come to de marsh. He was rat to de edge of Boudreaux & Clement's duckpond. Man, when dey saw dat hangin' aroun' glider comin', Boudreaux was so scared, he drop hees Rock 'n Roll Stage Plank an' Clement, him, he drop hees Honey Bun.

Dey bot' grab dere guns an' when Placide pass over de blind, dey bot' cut loose wit' everyt'ing dey had.

Boudreaux, him, only had 2 shots in hees twice-barrel shootsgun, but Clement had one of dem arromatic shootsgun (shoots tree shots from de same hole when

de game warden aint' roun', but five shots eef he ain't nowhere near), and let loose wit' all 5 shots.

Pooh-yi! Boudreaux say, "Clement!! what was dat?"

Clement say, "Non, me, I don't know. All I know is I must have caught him a good one, 'cause I made him drop Placide rat dere in de pond, I'll guarantee!"!

18. Boudreaux has a special fishing hole.

Down de bayou no one can catch any fish zep my cousin Boudreaux. Nobody can caught a stringer worth and ole cousin Boudreaux brings dem in by the ice chest full.

The game warden was a frien' of Boudreaux and axed eef he could go wit' him to his special place.

Boudreaux agreed and de next morning dey went to his special spot. No sooner dan dey stopped, Boudreaux pulled a stick of dynomite from under hees seat , lit it and t'road it in the water. Ka-Boom and the fish floated to the top for Boudreaux to scoop into his ice chest.

De game warden was shocked and said he could put Boudreaux in jail and forget where dey put de key.

Boudreaux jus't lit anoder stick of dynomite, t'rew it to the game warden, and said, "Are you gona talk or fish."

19. Big Elmo puts out de fire in Iraq.

Big Elmo was de fire chief in Mamou. Dey had a fire truck, tree firemens, and a firedog.

One day, after dat lunatic in Iraq set all dem fire in Kuwait, Big Elmo got him a viseet from one of dem big Salty Arabian Sheik-peoples, dat offer him five million dollars to come help put out dem fire.

Big Elmo pack up de whole fire department an' head over to de hairport in Lafayette where de Sheik's plane pick dem up. Big Elmo don't even stop, he drive rat on up into de plane an' eet take rat off.

When de plane eet lan' in Salty Arabia, Big Elmo drive de truck rat off de plane, across 10 mile of desert, an' rat smack dab into de middle of de firs' fire he come to, an' de truck stop in a big pile of sand.

Big Elmo, de tree firemens, and even de fire dog, all jomp out of de fire truck at de same time, an' start throwin' sand on dat oilwell fire jus' as fas' as dey could

'Bout 8 hour, de fire go out, an' de Salty Arabian Sheik-peoples came out to congratulate Big Elmo on heem putting out dat fire, an' to give him de five million dollars.

When he han' Big Elmo de case wit' all dem five million dollars in eet, he axe him, "Elmo, what you gonna do wit' dem five million dollars in a leettle town like Mamou? What you gone spend all dat money on?"

Elmo say, "De firs' t'ing ah'm gonna spend money on... is ah'm gonna put bout tree hundred dollars in some new brake for dat dam' truck, ah'll guarantee!"

20. Boudreaux tells Thibodeaux what to do when de policeman stops dare car.

Boudreaux and Thibodeaux were driving down de highway, drinking dare beer, when some flashing lights from a police car appeared in de rear-view mirror.

"Don't worry!" Boudreaux said to Thibodeaux. "Jus do zackly what I do, and everything will be alrat."

"First, we'll peel de labels off deese beer bottles and stick dem on our foreheads."

"Now, shove all de bottles under de seat and let me do all de talking!"

Dey did bot of dose t'ings den dey pull off to de side of de road.

De cop walks up to de side of de car and shined de light inside de car at de two drunks.

He axed, "Have you been drinking?"

"No sir," answered Boudreaux.

"I noticed you weaving back and forth on de road. Are you sure you haven't been drinking?" De cop axed.

"Oh no sir," Boudreaux answered. "We haven't had a drop tonight."

"Well den I have got to axe." De cop said, "What's dose t'ngs on your foreheads?"

"Oh dat's simple, officer." Said Boudreaux. "You see we are both trying to stop drinking, and now we're on de patch."

21. Boudreaux had trouble selling hees car.

Boudreaux tole Thibodeaux dat he was having trouble selling hees old car. Eet seems dat nobody wants to pay $1,500.00 for an old car weet' over 200,000 miles on eet.

Thibodeaux suggested dat Boudreaux he should roll de speedometer back.

Jus' a few days later Thibodeaux axed Boudreaux was he having any luck selling hees car.

Boudreaux said, "I decided not to sell eet."

Thibodeaux axed, "why?"

Boudreaux said, "Cause Eet only has 50,000 miles"...

22. A policeman stopped Boudreaux late one night.

Boudreaux left de bar room at closing time one night.

A policeman was across de street looking for anyone who might have had too much to drink.

When Boudreaux pulled out of de parking lot, de cop followed him down de street and stopped him.

De cop came up to Boudreaux's side window and shinned a light inside.

He said to Boudreaux, "I saw you leave dat barroom jus now, are you drunk?"

Boudreaux said, "Why no officer, do I have a ugly fat woman sitting next to me?"

23. Thibodeaux helps Boudreaux get his car ready for inspection.

Boudreaux needed to get hees car inspected.

He axed hees frien', Thibodeaux eef he would help him get ready for de inspection.

He tole Thibodeaux to get behind de car and tell him eef de turn lights worked.

Thibodeaux he got behind de car and said, "OK." Boudreaux he turned on de signal lights and axed Thibodeaux, "How dey doin?"

Thibodeaux said, "Well yea… well No… well yea well No… well yea"…

24. Boudreaux gets on de plan for Hawaii

When Boudreaux won the Louisiana lottery, he had more money dan he knew what to do w'it.

He got on a plane bound for Hawaii and he sit in de first class compartment.

When de stewardess came by checking tickets, she saw dat Boudreaux's ticket was for coach and axed him to move to de coach section.

Boudreaux tole her dat he won de lottery and was rich and could sit whereever he wanted.

De stewardess pleaded wit' Boudreaux and finally had to call de head stewardess for help.

Boudreaux tole de head stewardess de same t'ing. He said, "I won the lottery and I am rich, and I can sit anywhere I want."

De head stewardess soon became frustrated too. She called de pilot for help.

De pilot tole dem dat his wife was Cajun and he knew how to handle dis and bent over and whispered in Boudreaux's ear.

Boudreaux quickly got up and ran to de rear of de plane.

De stewardesses axed de captain what he said to him. The pilot said, "I tole him dat first class was not going to Hawaii

25. Boudreaux makes his firs' pairashoot jump.

Boudreaux joined de US Army and volunteered for de paratroopers. He went through all of de trainin and was ready to jomp.

Dey all got on a plane. Jus before dey was over de jomp zone, de sergeant tole dem not forget, "After you jomp, count to ten, take your rat han', put eet on your left shoulder and pull de cord for your parachute.

Eef de main chute don't work, take your left han', put eet on your rat shoulder and pull de cord for your reserve chute.

When you land on de ground dere will be a truck to pick you up and bring you back to base."

Boudreaux jomped out de plane over de jomp zone. He fell for 10 seconds, took hees rat han' put eet on hees left shoulder and pulled de cord for hees main chute.

Eet did not open.

He put hees left han' on hees rat shoulder and pulled de cord for hees reserve chute.

Eet deedn' open eider.

As he was falling to de ground, de udder paratroopers heard him screaming, "I'll bet dat de truck won't be dere eider."

26. Boudreaux and his friends complained every day about dere lunch.

Thibodeaux, Guidroz, and Boudreaux were working on a bridge. Every day at noon dey would open deir lunch pail and see de same lunch. Thibodeaux complained bout hees wife fixing him ham and cheese everyday.

Guidroz fussed dat hees wife fixed tuna fish salad sandwiches every day.

Boudreaux grumbled bout hees daily peanut butter and jelly sandwiches.

De next day, Thibodeaux opened hees lunch box to find ham and cheese sandwiches. He said, "Eef I get anoder ham and cheese sandwich, I'm gonna jomp off dis bridge."

Guidroz opened hees lunch box and found tuna fish. He said, "Eef I get anoder tuna fish salad sandwich, I'm gonna jomp off dis bridge."

When Boudreaux found dat he had peanut butter and jelly again. He said, "Eef I get anoder peanut and jelly sandwich, I'm gonna jomp off dis bridge too"...

De day after dey had all made de threat to jomp off de bridge, Thibodeaux opened hees lunch box to find a ham and cheese sandwich. He jomped off de bridge.

Guidroz found a tuna fish salad sandwich, and he jomped off de bridge.

Boudreaux jomped off de bridge when he saw hees peanut butter and jelly sandwich.

At de funeral, both Thibodeaux's and Guidroz's wives were crying. Dey could not understand why deir husbands deedn' tell dem to change deir sandwiches before jomping off de bridge.

Both wives spoke 'bout how dey would have been glad to make something deefferent eef de men just would have just tole dem something.

Boudreaux's wife was in de corner of de room showing real confusion.

She deedn' understand why he jomped, because he made hees own sandwiches for lunch.

27. Boudreaux applied for a job at the Baton Rouge Police Department.

My cousin Boudreaux was looking for a job. So he went down to de Baton Rouge Police Department.

He passed de written test fine, but was turned down when he flunked de physical.

De exam results showed dat he was allergic to donuts.

28. Cousin Boudreaux used to make big money.

My cousin Boudreaux used to make big money before he went to jail.

Eet was bout a quarter of an inch too big.

29. Boudreaux on de way home from work was stopped by a policeman.

Working 7 days straight on de offshore rig, Boudreaux and Thibodeaux were dog tired when dey drive back home to Pierre Part.

At de stop sign, Boudreaux slowed down, carefully looked both ways and took off.

A policeman saw dem and pulled dem over on de side of the road.

He axed Boo why he deedn' stop for de sign.

Boudreaux tole him, "I slowed down and was careful"

De cop tole Boudreaux to get out of de car. He den started hitting him wit' a stick. Boudreaux begged him to stop.

De cop said, "Now do you know de deefference between stopping and slowing down?"

Den, de cop tole Thibodeaux to get out of de car. He said he was going to grant hees wish.

When Thibodeaux got out de udder side of de car, de cop started hitting him wit' de stick, jus' like he did to Boudreaux.

Thibodeaux shouted, "What do you t'ink you are doing?"

De cop said. "I'm giving you your wish, because when you get bout 4 or 5 miles down de road you are gonna say I wish he would have hit me like dat."

30. While fishing, Boudreaux found a bottle floating in de water.

One day Boudreaux and Thibodeaux were out fishing.

Thibodeaux spotted a bottle floating in de water and picked eet up.

When he pulled out de cork, a great big genie appeared. De genie t'anked Thibodeaux for releasing him out of de bottle. He had been dere for hundreds of years and in return he would grant Thibodeaux one favor.

The genie tole Thibodeaux, "You can have anything in de world dat you want, but be careful because I can only grant you one wish."

Thibodeaux taught for a while and tole de genie dat he wanted all of de water in de lake to be turned into beer.

De genie said, "As you wish". Poof hees wish was granted and de genie disappeared.

Boudreaux got mad at Thibodeaux and tole him dat he should have wished for a lot of money and he could have bought all of de beer he would ever want.

Den he said, "Cause you were so stupid, we are now gonna have to pee in de boat."

31. Boudreaux picks up a pig off de highway

Boudreaux was riding along de highway when a truck passes wit' some pigs in eet.

One of de pigs fell out and Boudreaux stops to pick eet up.

A leettle while later, a state trooper stops and says, "Boudreaux, what you doin wit' dat pig?"

Boudreaux says, "A man passed by wid a truck full of pigs and dis one fell out. I was goin to try to catch up wit' de truck and give de man hees pig back."

De state trooper says "Boudreaux, dat man is long gone, why don't you just take dat pig to de zoo?"

Boudreaux said, "OK."

A couple of days later, de state trooper sees Boudreaux on de highway wit' de pig still in hees truck.

He stops Boudreaux and says, "Deedn' I tell you to bring dat pig to de zoo?"

Boudreaux says, "Mais, yea, but we had so much fun at de zoo, dat I t'ink we're gonna go to Astro World now!"

32. Boudreaux wanted to hide dat he was a Cajun while veesiting New York City

Cousin Boudreaux traveled to New York City.

A lot of de people laughed at him cause of de way he talked and acted.

He decided to try to talk and act like dem so dat dey would not laugh at him anymore.

Boudreaux went to a fancy restaurant wit' some people. Everyone ordered.

De waiter indicated dat eet was Boudreaux's turn to order.

Boudreaux ordered a hamburger, and said, "please cut de rice."

33. Boudreaux fussed at Clarence almos' every day.

Boudreaux lived across de bayou from Clarence. Boudreaux and Clarence did not like each other at all.

Dere was no bridge or udder easy way to cross de bayou so he two would argue by yelling across de bayou.

Boudreaux would often yell across de bayou to Clarence, "Clarence, eef I had a way to cross dat bayou, I would come beat you up!"

De threats continued for many years.

One-day de state built a bridge across de Bayou.

Boudreaux's wife, Marie, says, "Boudreaux, you've been talking bout going across dat bayou to beat up Clarence all dese years. Now dat dey have dat bridge, what are you waiting for?"

So Boudreaux decided eet was time to go see Clarence, so he started walking down to de bridge.

Just as he was getting ready to cross de bridge, he looks up at de sign on de bridge, reads eet, and goes back home.

When Boudreaux gets back home, Marie asks "Mais, Boudreaux, did you go beat up Clarence?"

Boudreaux said, "Mais no Marie, dat sign on at bridge says 'Clearance 13 feet 3 inches'. Mais, Marie, Clarence don't look dat big from across de bayou!"

34. Alphonse tole Boudreaux and Thibodeaux where de good fish are.

Pierre and Boudreaux went fishing in Pierre's boat, but dey deedn' do so good.

Dey came across Alphonse in a boat loaded wit' fish. Pierre axed Alphonse what hees secret was. Alphonse said, "Jes go out through dat pass over dere until de water gets fresh. Stop dere and drop yer line."

All excited, Pierre fired up de motor and headed through de pass.

When dey got a leettle ways out, he tole Boudreaux to fill up a bucket and taste de water. Boudreaux did jus' watt Pierre axed and said, "Eet's still salty, Pierre!"

Pierre went furder out and tole Boudreaux to taste de water again.

Boudreaux said de same thing, "Eet's still jus' as salty as before, Pierre!"

Dis went on for hours and eet was starting to get dark, and dey were in de middle of nowhere, when Pierre said to taste de water one last time.

Boudreaux replied, "But Pierre, dere's no more water in de bucket!"

35. Boudreaux and Pierre see de elevator in the city.

One day Boudreaux, hees wife Marie, and Boudreaux's frien', Pierre went to de city.

While Marie went shopping, Boudreaux & Pierre decided to go check out one of dem tall buildings.

Inside de building, Boudreaux & Pierre came to dese big golden doors.

Boudreaux says,"Wonda wat dees doors go too?"

So Boudreaux & Pierre stare at de doors for a few minutes until an old woman comes up to de doors.

She pushes a button near de door, de doors open, she goes inside, and de doors close.

Boudreaux & Pierre watch as numbers above de door start to change from "1" to "2" to "3", den de numbers stop a while den change again from "3" to "2" to "1." De doors open and a beauteeful young voluptuous woman walks out!

Boudreaux tells Pierre, "Mais you saw dat? Hurry up--let's go find Marie so we can put her in dere!"

36. Boudreaux meets his daughter's fiancée.

Boudreaux's daughter brings home her new fiancée to meet Boudreaux and Marie.

After dinner, Marie tells Boudreaux to find out bout de young man. Boudreaux invites de fiancée to de back room for a drink.

Boudreaux axed de young man, "So w'at are your plans?" "I am a scripture scholar", he replies.

"A scripture scholar. Hmmm," Boudreaux says, "Dats good, but what will you do to provide a nice house for my daughter to live in?"

"I will study," de young man replies, "and God will provide for us."

"And how will you buy her a beauteeful engagement ring?" Axed Boudreaux.

"I will concentrate on my studies," de young man replies, "God will provide for us."

"And children?" Axed Boudreaux. "How will you support de children?"

"Don't worry, sir, God will provide," replies de finance.

De conversation proceeds like dis, and each time Boudreaux questions, de young man insists dat God will provide.

Later, Marie asks Boudreaux, "Mais, how did eet go, Boudreaux?"

Boudreaux answers Marie by saying, "He has no job, and he has no plans, but de good news is ... he t'inks I'm God."

37. Boudreaux plans a valentine surprise for Marie.

For Valentines Day Boudreaux wanted to get Marie, hees wife, a real surprise. She had been wanting a milk bath for a long time.

So Boudreaux tole to hees frien' Pierre, he say, "Pierre, I wanna give Marie a milk bath for Valentine Day."

He den say, "Why don't you bring you cow over to da house and put me some milk in da bathtub."

Pierre answered, "Okay, Boudreaux. Dat milk, you want dat eet pasteurize?"

Boudreaux taught for a while, den said, "No, just so eet covers her belly, dat's all I want."

38. Cousin Boudreaux drives a taxi in Baton Rouge.

Boudreaux once had a job as a taxicab driver in Baton Rouge.

Soon after he started de job, he picked up a Texan on hees way to de airport. When dey passed by de LSU

football stadium, de Texan said, "What's that there?"

Boudreaux said, "Dat's de LSU Tiger Stadium."

De Texan said, "How long did it take y'all to build it?"

Boudreaux said, "Mais, bout five years."

De Texan said, "Oh, we've got a bigger one in Austin that only took one year."

As dey passed de state capitol, de Texan axed again, "What's that building?"

Boudreaux said, "Dat's de state capitol."

"And how long did it take y'all to build that?"

Boudreaux said, "Bout tree years."

De Texan said, "We've got one in Austin that only took six months."

Boudreaux had just bout enough of dis, you know. Den dey drove past de Mississippi River Bridge.

De Texan said, "How long did it take y'all to build that bridge?"

Boudreaux said, "I don't know. Eet wasn't dere dis morning."

39. Boudreaux meets a man on his Hawaiian vacation.

Boudreaux goes to Hawaii on vacation.

Down at de pool, a man sits down next to Boudreaux.

Boudreaux says, "Hey, how you doing? My name is Boudreaux and I'm here on vacation. My house caught eetself on fire. I got a leettle extra from de insurance company. Dat's how I came here on dis vacation."

"Well that's interesting," responded the man "I'm here from California. My house flooded. I used the extra insurance money for this vacation."

"Mais dats good," said Boudreaux "but let me axe you one ting. How de heck did you start de flood?"

40. Boo and Tee see a big hole in de woods

Boudreaux and Pierre were walking through de woods one day. Boudreaux grabbed Pierre by de arm pulling him back and said, "Whooee, Pierre, look at dat big hole you almost stepped in!"

Pierre looks down into de hole, and he says, "Whooee, Boudreaux, dat sure looks like a deep hole. I wonder how deep dat hole goes?"

Dey fined a rock, and throw eet into de hole, listening to see how long eet will take to hit de bottom. Dey don't hear anything.

Dey find a bigger rock and repeat de process, but still don't hear eet hit.

Pierre notices a railroad tie lying in de bushes, picks eet up and throws eet into de hole.

While dey listened for de railroad tie to hit de bottom, a leettle billy goat comes running out of de bushes. It runs rat between dem and jomps into de hole.

A few minutes later, deir frien', Thibodeaux comes walking through de bushes. Boudreaux says, "Hey Thibodeaux, what you doin' way out here in de woods?"

Thibodeaux answers, "Well I'm out here looking for my leettle billy goat."

Pierre says, "You want to hear sometin funny? De strangest ting just happens'. A leettle billy goat just came running out dem bushes, and jomped rat in dat deep hole rat dere."

Thibodeaux says, "Oh dat couldn't have been my billy goat. My goat was tied to a railroad tie back in dose bushes!"

41. Boudreaux splains watt hees sign means to Thibodeaux.

One day, Boudreaux had a sign in hees yard dat read "Boat for Sale."

Pierre came by and said, "Boudreaux ... tell me sometin ... why you got dat sign in de yard dat say 'Boat for Sale'? Mais, you ain't got no boat!"

Boudreaux replied "Mais no I don't have no boat, but see my car over dare by dat sign?"

Pierre responded "Mais yeah I see dat car."

Boudreaux said "And see my trailer over dare by dat sign?"

Pierre said "Mais yeah I see dat traylor."

Boudreaux said, "Mais Pierre, dey boat for sale, watts de matter wid you!"

42. Marie chooses an obituary for Boudreaux.

Boudreaux's wife, Marie, went to de local newspaper and said she wanted to put in de Obeetuary Column dat Boudreaux died.

De editor said dat eet would be $1.00 per word. Marie said, "Here's $2.00 - just put 'BOUDREAUX DIED'."

De editor said, "Mrs. Boudreaux, surely you want more dan dat."

Marie said, "Mais, no, just 'BOUDREAUX DIED'."

De editor said, "Well, Mrs. Boudreaux, I know you're a leettle upset. Bring yourself back tomorrow and you will probably t'ink of somethin' else."

Marie came back de next day, and said, "Yeh, I taught of somethin' else, put 'BOUDREAUX DIED, BOAT FOR SALE'."

43. Boo and Tee see a leettle green creature.

Pierre and Boudreaux were on a weekend hunt when dey witnessed a UFO landing.

As de leettle green creatures descended from de craft Pierre said, "Mais what's dat?"

Boudreaux answered, as he aimed hees gun: "I don't know me, Pierre. But you better go back to de camp and put some rice on."

44. Tee Boudreaux didn' have a bathroom in de house.

When Boudreaux was a leettle boy he was called "Tee Boudreaux." "Tee Boudreaux" lived wit' hees family in a house wit' no indoor plumbing.

Dey had an outhouse out in de back of de house. Hees daddy, Papa Boudreaux, wanted de best he could get for de Boudreaux family. So dey had a "two holer" outhouse so dat two people could "go" at de same time.

One day Tee-Boudreaux and Papa Boudreaux were both in de outhouse when Tee-Boudreaux saw hees Papa accidentally drop a quarter into de hole.

Tee-Boudreaux noticed hees Papa t'inking bout something for a while den he reach into hees pocket, pulled out a dollar bill, and drop eet into de hole where de quarter had gone.

Tee-Boudreaux saw dis and said, "Mais, Papa what you dropped dat dollar bill into dat hole for?"

Papa Boudreaux said, "Mais Tee-Boudreaux, I deedn' have de heart do send you down dere for just a quarter!"

45. Boudreaux wants a vasectomy.

After having deir 10th child, Boudreaux and Marie decided dat was enough.

So Boudreaux went to de doctor and tole de doctor dat he and Marie deedn' want to have any more children.

De doctor tole Boudreaux dat dere was a procedure called a vasectomy dat could fix de problem.

De doctor tole Boudreaux dat he was to go home, get a cherry bomb, light de fuse, put de cherry bomb in a can, den hold de can up to hees ear, and count to 10.

Boudreaux said, "I may not be de smartest man, but I don't see how putting a cherry bomb in a can next to my ear is going to help us not have any more children."

So Boudreaux and Marie drove to Texas to get a second opinion.

De Texas doctor was just bout to tell dem bout de procedure for a vasectomy when he figured out who he was dealing wit'.

So, de doctor tole Boudreaux to go home and get a cherry bomb, light de fuse, place de cherry bomb in a tin can, hold eet next to hees ear, and count to 10.

Figuring dat both doctors couldn't be wrong, Boudreaux went home, got a cherry bomb, leet de fuse, and put de cherry bomb in a can. He held de can up to hees ear and began to count on hees fingers, "1, 2, 3, 4, 5..." at which point he paused, placed de can between hees legs, and resumed hees counting weet' de fingers on hees udder han'.

46. Pierre axed Marie to fool around.

Boudreaux & Marie and Pierre & Cotile (two happily married couples) all decide to have a pedro game one night. So dey all meet at Boudreaux & Marie's house and begin playing cards.

After a couple of games, Boudreaux decides he needs to go to de bathroom, so he goes. Den Cotile decides to get more beer in de kitchen and she goes.

Pierre and Marie were still at de pedro table. Pierre, looking at Marie (Boudreaux's wife) tells her (Marie)

dat he t'inks she looks good and dat he would like nothing more dan to "fool around" wit' her.

Well, Marie gives in and tells Pierre dat eet will cost him.

Pierre asks "how much?" Marie says "$100.00." Pierre tells her dat is too much, being he has no job.

Den after a leettle while, Pierre agrees to pay her. Dey decide dat he will go over to her house de next morning while Boudreaux is at work.

So dey finish deir pedro game dat night, and Pierre goes over to Boudreaux's house just after Boudreaux leaves for work (not to see Boudreaux, no!!) and he and Marie spend de day togeder. Dey play around and gives her de $100.00 den leaves.

A leettle while later Boudreaux comes home and asks Marie eef Pierre came by today.

Marie was shocked, but couldn't tell a lie to Boudreaux and she says yes, "Pierre did come by."

Den Boudreaux asks eef Pierre gave her $100.00. Marie replies, "yes", while hesitating.

Boudreaux says, "dat good ole frien' of mine, Pierre; I knew I could count on him. Dis morning he came by work and borrowed $100.00 and said he'd have eet back by 5:00 PM."

47. Marie axed Boudreaux 'bout de note in his pocket.

One day while Marie was washing Boudreaux's clodes; she found a piece of paper in Boudreaux's pants pocket.

She opens up de paper and eet has de name "Mary Lou" written on eet.

Marie got real mad and stormed into de room where Boudreaux was and said, "Mais Boudreaux, you better explain to me who dis 'Mary Lou' is, rite now!"

Boudreaux said, "Mais Marie, don't you go worryin' bout dat. I went to de race track today and dat's de horse dat I bet on!"

Marie taught bout eet some and said "OK, but don't you ever let me find out dat you been messin' around wit' somebody else."

De next day, de phone rang and Marie answered eet. After a while she hung up de phone and den went over to Boudreaux carrying a big iron skillet. Marie hit Boudreaux on de side of de head wit' de skillet.

Boudreaux, rubbing hees head, said "Marie, mais what you done dat for?"

Marie said, "Mais, your horse just called!"

48. Boudreaux goes into a barroom in Texas.

One night, Michael Boudreaux stopped off in a barroom while he was in Texas.

He deen't know anyone, so to break de ice he axed a fellow at de bar eef he would like to hear an Aggie joke.

When the fellow stood up he must have been 6'5" an' weighed 280 pounds.

He said, "A'hm an Aggie and I don't like Aggie jokes and I especially don't like....Cajuns."

He pointed to the end of the bar and said, "That man down there is my friend. He weighs 295 pounds and is a professional football player. He's an Aggie too and he doesn't like Aggie jokes or Cajuns."

He Pointed to the other end of the bar and said, "That man over there is a professional wrestler. He weighs 320 pounds and is another Aggie friend of mine. He don't like Aggie Jokes and hates Cajuns even more."

He then asked Boudreaux if he wanted to tell an Aggie joke now.

Michael Boudreaux deedn't have to t'ink to long. He said, "I don't t'ink so. I don't wont to have to repeat eet tree times.

49. Boudreaux spoke to a curious Texan.

One day, Boudreaux was sitting on hees porch.

A truck drove up to Boudreaux's house and a man stepped out

De man introduced himself to Boudreaux. Den tole him dat he was from Texas, and dat he was getting some information bout land in de area.

De Texan said, "Mr. Boudreaux, how much land do you have here where you live?"

Boudreaux said, "Mais, I have bout two acres."

De Texan said, "That's not much land." Back in Texas where I'm from, it takes me just about all day to drive my truck down my driveway to my house."

Boudreaux t'inks bout what de Texan said for a while and den he responds, "Yeah, I used to have a truck like dat too."

50. Boudreaux was stopped for speedin' while Marie was in de car.

One day Boudreaux was driving de car wit' Marie in de passenger seat.

A policeman pulled Boudreaux's car over to de side of de road. De policeman came up to de window of de car next to Boudreaux. Den de policeman tole Boudreaux dat he was speeding and dat he would have to give Boudreaux a ticket.

Boudreaux tole de policeman dat he was not speeding.

Boudreaux den turns to Marie and says, "Mais, Marie you was watching me. Tell de officer eef dats true, was I speeding?"

Marie turns to de officer and says, "Mais officer, I can't tell you eff my husband was speeding or not, cause I don't pay attention to him when he's been drinking!"

51. Boudreaux got heem a new chain saw.

Boudreaux bot heemself a new chain saw. He was havin' a real good time cutting off all of de low branches on de trees around hees house.

Soon he got heemself brave and started swinging the saw around to geet the higher branches. Before yo know it he cut off hees ear.

Hees frien' Thibodeaux helped heem look for his ear. Den Thibodeaux he say, "Here eet is Boudreaux. I found yo ear."

Boudreaux looked quickly and he say, "Dats not ma ear. Ma ear had a peensil in eet."

52. Boudreaux's golf treesom become a twosom.

Boudreaux decided to go play a game of golf with hees good frien's Guidry and Hebert one morning. He promised Marie dat he would be home in time for lunch.

Well, lunchtime came and went, and no Boudreaux. Mid afternoon came and go, still no Boudreaux. Suppertime passed, and Boudreaux finally shows up about an hour later. Marie is, of course, jus' a leetle bit mad.

"Boudreaux, where in heck you been? You say you gonna be home by lunch, and here it is dark time, and you jus now gettin' home!"

Boudreaux says, "Marie, don' get on my case. My good frien', Guidry, died on de golf course dis morning."

Marie says, "Oh, Boudreaux, I'm so sorry. I can understan' now; makin' funeral arrangements for your frien, and all. I understan' why you late."

Boudreaux says, "Funeral arrangements. What arrangements? It was 'Hit de ball, drag Guidry. Hit de ball, drag Guidry. It took me and Hebert all day to finish the game!"

53. Boudreaux gets lost easy.

Ma cousin Boudreaux is a man dat gets lost real easy. I hear one time dat he got loss in a phone booth.

When I hear dat him an hees son T-Boy was gone hunting' in de woods, I got to worry. I tole him "Eef you get you-self lost, what you got to do is shoot in de air tree times, wait 5 minute an shoot tree time again. Keep doing dat til some-one finds you."

Well shore nuff, dey got dem self lost, so Boudreaux him he start shoot in de air.

He shoots tree time wait five minute shoot again an he did dat four time.

Den he said to T-Boy, "I hope dat some one finds us soon, cause I'm bout to run out of arrows!"

54. Boo, Tee, and Broussard been on dis island for five years.

Boudreaux, Thibodeaux & Broussard been on dis island for five long years.

One day Broussard was walking along da beach when he found dis bottle.

He brought teet to da camp dey built. He opened eet. A genie popped out and said, "I will you grant 3 wishes and since dere are 3 of y'all, you each will get 1 wish. Since you found me, Broussard, you get de first wish."

Broussard said, "I am from Houma and I wanna go back home." Poof, den he was back home in Houma.

Thibodeaux said, "I am from Napoleonville and I wanna go back home." So den Poof and Thibodeaux was back home.

Boudreaux, him, he had to t'ink a while. He said, "You know cher I am kinda lonley, I wish my 2 podnas were back here!"

55. Thibodeaux roasted a pig at hees house.

One time, ole' Thibodeaux had a cochon de lait (Cajun Pig Roast) in de back of hees house.

Well, Broussard saw dat one of Thibodeaux's children was running around wit' a real strange outfit.

Broussard said "Hey, Thibodeaux, wot dat yor baby got on heesself?"

Thibodeaux said, "Man, dats a Pampers, cher (shah)!"

Broussard said "Wot you mean a Pampers?"

Thibodeaux said "It's like a diaper, but you don' got to washeet, you don' got to fol'eet - you jus' tro'ed away."

Broussard said "WHOO MAN! I need ta gots me some o' dem Pampers!"

De next weekend, ole' Broussard was having a crawfish boil in de back of hees house. Thibodeaux said, "Whoo man, looks like you gots some a dem Pampers on yor babies!"

Broussard said "Yeh, I love dem Pampers, cher. You don' gots to wash 'em, you don' gots to fol'em, you jus' tro'ed 'em away."

Thibodeaux said "Wall den, you need to change dat Pampers on dat little Pierre."

Broussard said "No I don'."

Thibodeaux said "An yes you do!" Broussard went and picked up Pierre and shook him a little and again said "No, I don'!"

Thibodeaux said, "Look at dat! He got de shoo-shoo come out de back o' de Pampers. He got de shoo-shoo come out de front o' de Pampers. He got de shoo-shoo run all down hees legs!

Man, WHY you not change dat pampers?"

Broussard said "CAUSE! De box says eets good for 18 to 23 pounds!"

56. Thibodeaux's big fat wife was gonna fix his favorite meal.

One time, ole' Thibodeaux wanted hees favorite meal, blue crabs.

Hees Big Fat Wife said "Allrat Thibodeaux, I tole' you wot I'm gonna do. I'm goin down to de bay an' caught you some blue crabs, cher. An den I'm gonna fix you de bes' boiled blue crab you eva did have."

Thibodeaux said "Whoo, Big Fat Wife, dat would be mo' betta dan blackberry wine, cher!"

De next morning, Thibodeaux's Big Fat Wife got ready to go catch some blue crabs down at de bay.

Thibodeaux said "Wot time you are goin to be back home, Big Fat Wife?" She said "I'll be home in time to clean an cook dem crabs for suppa, Thibodeaux."

All day long Thibodeaux waited for hees Big Fat Wife to get home. eet got to be bout five o'clock, and Thibodeaux taught "My Big Fat Wife mus' be catchin a big mess a dem blue crabs or she woulda been home by now."

Den eet got to be bout nine o'clock and Thibodeaux's Big Fat Wife still wasn't home.

Thibodeaux taught "Whar in de worl' be my Big Fat Wife?"

It got to be midnight, and Thibodeaux's Big Fat Wife was still missing, so Thibodeaux decided to call de Sheriff.

Thibodeaux said "Sheriff, my Big Fat Wife wen' down to de bay to caught me some blue crabs dis mornin, but she still not home."

De Sheriff said "OK Thibodeaux. We'll go out to fin' yor Big Fat Wife."

At one AM, Thibodeaux heard a knock at de door. eet was de Sheriff. Thibodeaux said "Sheriff, did you fin' my Big Fat wife?"

De Sheriff said "Thibodeaux, I got you some good news an I got you some bad news."

Thibodeaux said, "Oh no. Gimme de bad news firs'."

De Sheriff said, "Weeall, Thibodeaux, we foun yor Big Fat Wife. She dun fell into de bay an got drown."

Thibodeaux said "Oh my po' ole' Big Fat Wife."

"But you know wot?" de Sheriff went on, "We foun' TWENTY SEVEN o' de BIGGEST Blue Crab you eva SAW hangin on her."

Thibodeaux said "Oh Sheriff, dat's not good news!"

De Sheriff said "No Thibodeaux! De good news is we're gonna run her ag'in in bout a hour!"

57. It takes a Cajun to help de good ole boys get de mule into de barn.

Dese two good ole' boys from Beaumont bought a new mule, but had trouble getting him in deir barn.

Every time dey would get de mule to de door, hees ears would brush de top of de doorway and he'd start kicking and go wild.

Finally, dey decided dat de best way to solve de problem is to jack up de barn. So, dey go out and get a half dozen jacks.

De two Texans were scrambling from jack to jack to trying to get de barn raised when Pierre LeMieux walks up.

"Watcha doin?" Pierre axed.

Billy Bob said, "Wer' raisin thuh barn, yuh stoopid Cajun."

"Why you do dat?"

Billy Bob said, "Cause thuh mule's ears keep touchin' thuh doorway when we try to put him in dis-here barn and he goes haf-crazy wild. He kicked Ernest Wayne plumb in thuh haid twicet already."

Pierre said, "Why come you don' just dig de hole in de doorway? Dat way he's got to go down when he gets to de do'r an hees ear don't touch nutin."

"Ya stoopid Cajun," Ernest Wayne chimes in. "It's hees ears at's too long, not hees laigs!"

58. De motor fell off de boat.

Boudreaux and Thibodeaux went to Henderson to go fishing. Dey rented a boat and motor and took off. Dey deedn' go far when dey hit a stump and de motor fell off in bout ten feet of water.

Boudreaux looked at Thibodeaux and say, "What we gonna do?"

Thibodeaux looked at Boudreaux and he say, "We got to go down and get de motor, dat's all dere is to eet."

Thibodeaux say to Boudreaux, "You go down dere and get de motor, I'll throw dis rope over de side so you can pull eet eef you have trouble."

Boudreaux say, "O.K." and he dive in and went straight to de bottom.

De water was clear and Thibodeaux was watching Boudreaux from de boat.

A few seconds later he sees Boudreaux on de bottom pulling de starter rope on de motor trying to start eet.

Thibodeaux say, "Look at dat stupid idiot. He oughta know he can't start de motor dat way."

Thibodeaux leans over de side of de boat and shouts into de water, "Boudreaux, CHOKE eet! CHOKE eet!"

59 Thibodeaux takes hees cat to de Bet.

One day, Thibodeaux noticed hees cat looked kinda sick, So he phoned up de local Vet, Doctor LeBlanc.

Once Doctor LeBlanc got dere, he said, "well, show me da cat."

Thibodeaux han's him de cat, and Dr. LeBlanc takes a look, he stroked hees han's along de rat side of de cat,

den he stroked hees han's along de left side of de cat and finally gives a little touch to de cat's head and tail.

"Well?...What could eet be, asks Thibodeaux." "Looks like you called me over for nothing, seems da cat just got a hold of some bad catnip or somethin'," replied de Doctor.

"Well, How much to I owe ya?" asks Thibodeaux.

Well, I won't charge ya nothin for my services, but eet'll be 500 dollars for de CAT-SCAN

60 De Cajun and Redneck raccoon meet up w'it each udder.

One morning a Cajun raccoon met up wit' a redneck raccoon from Mississippi.

Dey were walkin' along peacefully when all of a sudden, "CLACK" both of'em got caught in some traps.

Well as soon as de traps went off dey could hear some huntin' dogs approaching.

"Quick! chew ya paw off and we can escape," says de Cajun Coon. So de Cajun coon chews hees paw off and starts runnin' for hees life.

After bout a minute or so, he notices dat de Redneck ain't behind him...worried, he back tracks all de way back to de traps and finds de Redneck still in de trap!

De Cajun coon shouts, "What you doin'? I tole you to chew your paw off! Hurry up, de dogs almost here!"

De red neck replies, "Dangit! Dat don't work! I done chewed three of my paws off and I'm STILL stuck in dis trap!"

61. Courville finds out w'at archritis is.

Dare was da time Courville was on an airplane. He'd never flown on a airplane before. He deedn' even know dey assigned you to a seat.

He did got hees boarding pass and he got had hees seat number and dey had him sitting rat next to a Catholic priest.

He knew he was a Catholic priest because he had a collar on. (Da white-collar dat dey wear, every time dey go someplace so dey can get da clerical discount.)

So Courville was sitting on da plane rat next to da priest and he found out dat you could order beer on airplanes, so he ordered him a beer, man, and he drank da beer real fast and he ordered him anoder beer and drank eet fast.

It kind of bodered da priest dat dis guy was drinking beer so fast. Courville he ordered him a tird one and drank eet fast too.

Well, soon as da beer started working, he started cutting up wit' da stewardess. Eet really bodered da priest a lot dat all dis was going on.

Finally de plane got to cruising altitude, and man, Courville jomp up in hees seat, and he looked at da priest.

He said, "Fader, I know you aren't a medical doctor or anyt'ing like dat, but, is dare any chance, you would know what causes archritus?"

Da priest t'inks to hisself, dis is my chance to get him to understand some tings. He say, "Oh yes my son, I do know what causes arthritis."

He say, "arthritis is caused by excessive drinking and improper behavior wit' women."

"Poo Yie," Courville said, "I was just wondering."

He say, "Sitting in dat terminal dis morning, I read in dat US and A Today newspaper, eet said da Pope got archritus."

62. Cormier was chased by a policeman on de road.

Cormier was driving down da road and he look in hees rear view mirror and he see dis state trooper rat behind him. Man he take off full blass, going bout 80 mile an hour.

Da state trooper say, "I can't let him get away wit dis, you know." So he chase him down, he pull him over and look at hees license.

He say, "Mr. Cormier, I followed you for bout twelve mile. He say, "For ten of dem mile everything was fine, all of a sudden you take off! What happened?"

Cormier said, "Well, I saw you in my rear view mirror and I got to t'inking, bout tree years ago my wife run away wit a state trooper". He said, "I taught dat was you bringing her back!"

63. De kids keep waking Pawpaw Boudreaux.

Den dare was da time Grandpa Boudreaux was visiting hees son's house one Sunday afternoon.

Sitting down watching da Saints on TV, da next thing you know, he fall asleep, dat's cause eets easy to fall asleep when da Saints on TV.

Course dey hadn't even been on TV lately. Incidentally, dat was da problem dey had wit da Superbowl. Dey deedn' t'ink da camera would work; dey hadn't been used in so long.

So anyway, he's watching TV and he fall asleep and after he sleep awhile, he feel a tug on hees pant leg and he jomps up.

Eets one of hees grandson, and da boy say, "Pawpaw, Pawpaw, can you make a noise like a frog?" And he say, "Go away son, I'm trying to sleep."

A little while later he feels anoder tug on hees pant leg. eet's anoder grandson and he say, "Wake up Pawpaw. Pawpaw, can you make a noise like a frog?"

He say, "Leave me alone, son, I'm trying to sleep."

Little while later, dare's anoder tug and eets hees two year old grandson, da youngest one, he say, "Pawpaw, Pawpaw, can you make a noise like a frog?"

So he pick up da boy, he puts him on hees lap. He said, "Son, he say, what's wrong wit you and your broders today?"

He said, "Well Pawpaw," he say, "Last night we heard Mama and Daddy talking, dey said when Pawpaw croaks, we going to Disney World."

64. Guidry's papa wanted some 4x2's

Den dare was da time dat Guidry boy went to de LeMieux (In French dat means de best) lumberyard. He said he wanted to buy some 4 by 2's.

Mr. Pierre, de owner say, "Well, we don't have any 4 by 2's", he say, "We have some 2 by 4's."

De Guidry boy say, "Well, my Poppa's really kinda particular, I better go check wit him."

Bout an hour later de Guidry boy come back. Mr. Pierre say, "You figured out what you want?" He said, "Yeah," he said, "My Poppa said since you outta dem 4 by 2's, he t'ink he can make dem 2 by 4's fit."

Mr. Pierre said, "Well, okay. How long do you want dem?"

The boy say, "Oh, he's gonna need 'em for a long time, he plans on building a house!"

65. Ms Robicheaux sent her boy to de priest.

Den dare was da time Ms. Robicheaux was scared dat her youngest boy wouldn't turn out real good. So she talked to da priest. Da priest said "Send him over and I'll counsel wit' him."

Now she send da twelve year old boy to meet wit da priest.

Da priest wasn't sure how to get t'ings going when de boy sat down. He looked at de young man and said, "Son, where is God?"

Da boy he deedn' say anything.

De priest again said, "Son, where is God?" He still got no response.

Da priest by dis time is getting a little aggravated.

He say, "Son, where is God?"

Man, da boy got up, he ran out da office and ran all da way home and hid in da closet.

A couple hours later hees broder find him hiding in da closet. He say, "Eno, what you doing in da closet?"

De boy say, "Man, I'm not xactly sure. But, God's missing and dey t'ink we got him!"

66. General Dupuis also had a plan for de Gulf War.

In da Gulf War, General Schwartzkoff was in charge of tings, but he deedn' have da only plan for winning da war. General Dupuis had a plan too.

General Dupuis' plan was to bring 500 Cajuns. He figured he could get em mostly from St. Martin Parish, mainly, Cecilia and Arnaudville.

De general would let dem bring dey own gun and instead of 500,000 troop, all he had to do was bring dem 500 Cajun to Saudi Arabia.

On da way over dare, dey just had to convince dem dat dose Iraqis made a good gumbo!

And once dey got dem to da Iraqi border, dey just had to turn 'em loose and tell dem dat de limit was one, don't shoot at night, and da season was closed!

He said, "eet would've for shore ended da war in tree day!"

67. Angelle and Trahan wanted to mark de spot for de good fishin' spot.

Angelle and Trahan dey wanted to go fishing in da Atchafalaya Basin. Neider one of dem had a boat, so dey rent a boat at one of dose boat place.

Man, dey go out, dey find dis spot, dey-catching fish like crazy.

Dey'd cast a line and pull in a fish, cast a line, pull in a fish. Sometime da fish jus' jomp in da boat as soon as dey cast a line.

Da boat's almost ready to sink; dey caught so many fish. But now it's time dey got to go in.

Angelle said, "You know, Trahan, we had a really good day today."

Trahan said, "Yep."

He say, "You know, Angelle, we might wanna come back here one day."

Angelle said, "Yep."

Trahan finally said, "You know, Angelle, in case we wanna come back here, we ought to mark da spot.

Angelle pull out hees pocketknife, he leans over to da side da boat and he proceeds to carve a "X" on da side da boat.

Trahan said, "Mais, Angelle, what da heck you do?"

Angelle said, "Trahan, we been talking for a long time bout marking da spot. I'm marking da spot."

Trahan said, "You idyut! How you know we gonna get dis same boat next time?"

68. Boudreaux sat next to a distinguished looking gentleman on the plane

Boudreaux got on an airplane in New Orleans headed for Chicago.

As he sat down he introduced heemself to de well dressed gentleman dat was sitting next to heem. He said, " Ma name is Boudreaux. I'm from Pierre Part and when I don't work on de oil rig, I catch crawfish for a living."

The gentleman told him dat he was a big time attorney from Chicago.

Boudreaux said, "W'it a job like that yo mus' be pretty smart."

De gentleman responded, "Yes, I am very intelligent.

How would you like to play a little game with me to pass the time away on this trip?'

Boudreaux, he say, "W'at kinda game you want to play?"

The gentleman said, "You ask me any question that you want. If I can't give you the correct answer, I'll give you a hundred dollars. Then I'll ask you a question.

To be fair with you since, I have a lot more education, you only pay me one dollar if you can't answer my question. You go first."

Boudreaux said, "What has ten eyes, fourteen legs, two tails and lives on the bottom of Bayou Black?"

The gentleman said, "I do not know the answer to that one. Here is your one hundred dollars as we agreed. By the way, what is it?"

Boudreaux replied, "I donno, here is you dollar."

70. De young quarterback listened to de coach

Breaux Bridge was playing Cecilia in football and eet was almost halftime, when da score was nutin-nutin.

Man and da starting quarterback for Breaux Bridge get hurt, so dey send in da second team quarterback.

Tree play later, he get hurt.

Man, da coach had to find a leetle tirteen year old freshman, tird team quarterback on da bench, dat never play before.

He say, "Son, come here. I need to put you in da game."

Den he say, "All I want you to do is hold dis t'ing, tied jus' like eet is till halftime den we can regroup." He say, "Jus' go out dare, run tree time and kick! Don' do nutin else. You hear?"

De lettle freshman say, "Okay, Coach."

So man, he go out, he's in da shotgun. Dey snapping da ball, he run around left end and go nineteen-yard.

De second play dey snap da ball again, man, he run around rat end for tirty-one yard.

De next play from scrimmage dey snapping da ball, he run eet rat up da middle, down to da one yard line. Man, dey tackle him.

Den man, de next play, de snap him da ball, he's in de shotgun and he kick da most beauteeful punt you ever saw in your life.

Den he come walking off da field and da coach finally grab him.

He say, "Son, answer me one question. What were you t'inking when you kicked da ball?"

He said, "Mais, I was t'inking, boy we sure got a stupid coach!"

70. Boudreaux and Hebert help build an airport in Breaux Bridge.

Did you hear dey were gunna put an airport in Breaux Bridge?

For real?

You lying?

Dey hired Hebert and Boudreaux to figure out how to position da runway.

Dey tole Hebert and Boudreaux, dat dey had to measure how high everything was in Breaux Bridge.

Dey even made Hebert da boss.

So Hebert and Boudreaux got a hundred-foot tape and dey start measuring. (Dat's all you need when you gonna measure da high of tings in Breaux Bridge, is a hundred foot tape.)

Dey measure da house, da tree, da barn and when dey got into town, dey measure all da building.

Dey measure city hall and when dey came to da flag pole in front of city hall dey weren't sure how dey were gonna measure eet.

So finally Hebert say, "Boudreaux, I got eet figured out."

He say, "Gimme me da end of da tape, I'm gonna tie eet to my belt loop and I'm gonna climb da pole.

You hold da tape down here and we'll know how high eet is."

So Hebert got bout half way up da flagpole and he slid back down.

He start climbing again, got 'bout half way up and he slid down again.

Boudreaux say, "Hebert, get out of my way, let me show you how to do dis."

Den he hooks da tape to hees belt loop, gets bout tree-fours of da way and he slide down.

When he's sliding down, he's looking down and when he hits da ground, he say, "Hebert, I got eet."

Hebert say, "Boudreaux, you deedn' go much higher dan me, what you mean, you got eet?"

He say, "I figured out what we gonna do."

Boudreaux say, "Look at dis flagpole. It's just a metal pole and eet's welded to an iron-metal plate, dey got four hole in da metal plate and dey got four bolt dat bolted to da cement."

He den say, "All we're gonna do is take da four bolt out, and we're gonna lay eet on da ground and we gonna measure eet."

Hebert say, "Hot-doggit, Boudreaux. Dat's why dey put me in charge of da operation.

Dey don't gotta know how long eet is, dey gotta know how high eet is!"

71. Boudreaux gave his parrot a cold lesson.

Boudreaux went to de pet shop to buy a parrot. He found a buteeful bird. He was so proud he couldn't wail to get home and show hees wife Marie.

When he got de parrot home he noticed dat eet had a fowl mouth and cussed all de time.

Boudreaux tole de bird to stop Da cussing and fowl language.

De bird continued and would not stop no matter what Boudreaux said.

Finally, Boudreaux got mad and put de bird into de freezer. Bout five minutes later, Boudreaux felt guilty and let de bird out of de freezer.

De parrot said dat he would not say anoder cuss word again. De parrot said he did have one question though.

When Boudreaux agreed to answer, De parrot axed, "What did dat chicken in de freezer do?"

74. Thibodeaux knows what a real echo is.

Thibodeaux was visiting de Texas hill country jus' outside of Austin.

Dare he met a bragging Texan who bet him dat he could make de longest echo known in the hill country.

Thibodeaux accepted de challenge, an' de Texan hollered, "HELLO." Den de echoes come back. HELLO – HEllo – hello.

Thibodeaux tole de Texan dat dose echoes was not nearly as good as de ones in da Atchafalaya swamp.

De Texan tole Thibodeaux, "its impossible to make an echo in a swamp."

Thibodeaux said, "Come to Louisiana, I'll showyu."

Dey went to de swamp; Thibodeaux paddled quite a ways. He stopped. He Shouted, "BOUDREAUX."

A few seconds later, dey heard, "OVER HERE, OVER Here, OVER here, Over here, over here.

73. Pierre knows how to get his money back at de casino.

Boudreaux and Pierre decided to go to de casino one day. Boudreaux tole Pierre as dey entered, "Alrat Pierre, we'll meet here in an hour, ok?"

Well, when dey were done, Boudreaux was broke, but Pierre had a bucket full of quarters.

"Man, were you got all dem quarters?" axed Boudreaux.

Pierre, leaning close, whispered, "Man, I don't want to say dis too loud, but you see dat game over dere, every time I put in a dollar, eet gives me four quarters!"

74. Boudreaux paints de church.

Fader Trahan axed Boudreaux eef he would paint de church.

Boudreaux agreed and began to study de job. He got to t'inking dat eef he mixed de paint wit' half water, he would have enough to paint hees house too, and nobody would know de deefference.

Boudreaux mixed de paint wit' half water. He painted de church and was almost finished wit' hees house when eet started to rain.

He cried out loud, "Oh Lord please don't let eet rain cause everybody will know what I did w'it de paint."

All of a sudden, dere was thundering and lightening, and a loud voice from de heavens said, "You thinner, you thinner, repaint, repaint and thin no more."

75. Amos was a real bell ringer.

One time, dare was dis man name Amos Cadiere, an' he brought himself to town to try an' find a job

Amos had loss both of hees arms to de alligators in de Atchafalaya (dat's a river an' swamp basin both) when he was younger an' hees pa-pa ran low on gater bait.

Amos look an' look, but couldn't find one job dat he could do.

Desperate, Amos he look in dem classyfried ad in de newspaper. Dare he saw where Fader Deophile at de Catholic church was looking for a bell ringer for de mass on Sundays.

Amos went see Fader Deophile, an' axe him for de job.

Fader Deophile say, "Mais, Amos you don't got no arms. How you going to ring dat bell, auh?

Amos say, "Fader, eef I can figure out a way to done dat, can I have de job? I can't find no udder work, an' ah'm getting' hungry, dere."

Fader Deophile say ok. So Amos went up in de bell tower an' stood dere for a good 5 minutes, tryin' to figure out how to ring dat bell.

Finally, Amos ran rat at de bell an' hit eet wit' hees face. Got a real nice tone out of de bell too. He came down, an' de priest give him de job.

De fader tole Amos, "Be here at 6 a.m. on Sunday morning to ring de bell for mass."

Bright an' early on Sunday, Amos show up to ring de bell. He climb up in de tower, an' rat at 6 o'clock, he start ringing de bell. Six times he ring de bell an' hit eet wit' hees face.

Seven a.m. mass, an' Amos rang de bell 7 times. Eight a.m. mass, 9-a.m. mass, until he got to de 10-a.m. mass.

By dis time, Amos' face was so swelled up he couldn't see a darn t'ing. When he ran at de bell, he miss eet complete, an' he fell out de belltower an' kill himself on de sidewalk below.

A crowd gadered, an' dis man say, "Mais, poor man! He dead, yeah! Does anybody know who he is?"

An ole woman in de crowd lean over an' say, "I don't know de name, but de face sure ring a bell"

76. Amos's brother was a real bell ringer too.

Bout 2-week's later, Amos' broder, ti-Caille (pronounced tee-kye) come to town, just like Amos did.

Ti-Caille got de same problem wit' hees arms dat Amos had. (Deir pa-pa ran low on gator bait a good bit in dem days, you see.)

He went to see de priest just like Amos did, an' ended up getting de job de same way.

On Sunday morning, ti-Caille show up an' did just like hees broder did de week before. An' by 10 a.m. mass, ti-Caille couldn't see no better dan Amos did de week before.

He run at de bell, an' he miss dat complete. Out de belltower he fell, and crunch, he kill himself in almos' de axzak same place Amos did.

A crowd gadered. Dis man say, mais, jamais-vie! (never-life) the poor man! He done kill himself dead! Does anybody know who he is?

De same lady from de week before lean over, take one look at ti-Caille all smash up on de banquette (dat's a sidewalk) an' she say, I don't know de name, but he's a dead ringer for de guy dat was here last week.

77. Cousin Boudreaux wants a drumstick for everyone.

Cousin Boudreaux was trying to cross a centipede wit' a turkey, so dat dare would be enouf drumsticks for everybody at t'anksgivin.

78. Boudreaux and Thibodeaux studded for the LSU entrance exam.

Ole Boudreaux and Thibodeaux decided to goin de LSU Tiger football team.

When dey practiced wit' de team de coaches said dey were good enough to play.

Before dey could join de team, dey would have to pass de enterance exam to get into college.

Boudreaux and Thibodeaux started to study for de test. Dey had a test booklet wit' sample questions to study.

Boudreaux looked over to Thibodeaux and said, "Tee, dis question number 14 sure got me stumped, eet says Old McDonald had a Blank."

Tee said, "Boo, you must be pretty dumb, everybody knows dat Old McDonald had a farm."

Den Boudreaux say, "OK den, how do you spell farm."

Thibodeaux busted out laughing and said, "You aren't jus dumb you're jus plain stupid. Everybody knows how dat you spell farm, eet's E I E O."

79. Boudreaux bot his firs' mirror.

A long time ago, dey used to be peddlers who went up and down de bayou in deir pirogues selling deir wares.

When Pierre, de peddler, came by Boudreaux's house, he showed him a mirror.

Boudreaux had never seen a mirror before. As he looked into eet he said out loud, "Such a likeness of my papa dat I never saw before.

Boudreaux axed how much dis was.

Pierre tole him two dollars. Boudreaux said he don't have two dollars in hees pocket.

All of a sudden Boudreaux remember Marie's cookie jar. He took two dollar from Marie's cookie jar and paid Pierre.

Later, as he was admiring de likeness of hees Papa in de mirror dat Pierre sole him, Marie came up de bayou.

Boudreaux quickly hid de mirror under de bed so dat Marie would not know dat he used her money from de cookie jar.

As de day went on, Boudreaux would slip out of de room, every once in a while, and sneak anoder peak at de mirror.

Marie noticed dat Boudreaux was slipping in and of de room.
She was starting to wonder what de ole fool was up too.

When Boudreaux left de house, Marie quickly went into de bedroom to search and find whatever had Boudreaux's attention earlier. She found de mirror.

She also had never seen a mirror before. When she looked into de mirror and remarked, "Oh, so dis is de hussey dat de ole man is foolin around wit'."

80. Boudreaux and Thibodeaux were talking 'bout de taste of nutria.

Thibodeaux and Boudreaux were walking along the bayou when dey saw a nutria.

Thibodeaux axed eef Boudreaux if he had ever ate any nutria.

Boudreaux answered, "shore I have."

Thibodeaux axed, "Den w'at do it taste like?"

Boudreaux replies, "sorta like owl."

81. Thibodeaux went to look at de bull.

Thibodeaux and Boudreaux had a farm. Dey had all kinds of animals on de farm but dey needed a Bull to complete de herd.

Boudreaux read bout a Bull sale in New Mexico, so he sent Thibodeaux down to New Mexico to check eet out.

After tree days looking, Thibodeaux found de perfect Bull.

He went to de local Western Union to send Boudreaux de following telegram: "Boudreaux, come and get de bull in New Mexico", your frien' Thibodeaux.

The Western Union cleark tole Thibodeaux dat he only had enough money for one word.

After t'inking bout dis, Thibodeaux sent de following message to Boudreaux: "COMFORTABLE."

De Western Union guy said "Comfortable", why comfortable. Thibodeaux replied, well you see, my frien' Boudreaux reads slow: COM-FOR-TA-BLE.

82. De moder crawfish teach de babees.

A baby crawfish and eets moder were walking along a ditch when de baby crawfish dat had gone ahead, comes flying back down de ditch.

De moder followed and axed, "What is de matter?"

De baby crawfish answers, "Look at dat big thing rat dere." De moder says "Don't worry bout dat; eet is just a cow." So dey keep walking.

Den de baby crawfish comes flying down again. De moder axed again, "What is de matter?"

De baby says look at dat thing rat dere. De moder says "Dat is just a dog; eet will not hurt you," so dey kept walking.

Den suddenly de moder goes flying by de baby crawfish. De baby crawfish axed eets moder what's wrong.

De moder said, "Run! Dat's a Cajun and dey eat anything."

83. De Deeference between Cajun and udder zoo's

Q. What's de deefference between Cajun zoos and udder zoos?

A. In front of each exhibit, udder zoos have a plaque wit` de name of de animal, eets habitat, etc.

Cajun zoos have a plaque wit' de name of de animal and eets recipe.

84. Boudreaux can't pass up a bargain at de drug store.

Ole Boudreaux saw suppositories on sale 12 for a dollar at de drug store.

He couldn't pass up a deal like dat, an got a dozen to take home wit him. Dat night, he ate all 12 of dem.

He tole Thibodeaux dat he had got 12 suppositories on sale at de drugstore.

Thibodeaux said, "I hope you're feeling better, what did you do wit dem?"

Boudreaux said, "I ate dem. What do you t'ink I did wit dem? Put dem in my butt?"

85. De 911 operator confused Boudreaux.

Boudreaux's wife Marie passed away and Boudreaux called 911.

De 911 operator tole Boudreaux dat she would send someone over rat away.

"Were do you live?" Axed de operator.

"At dat end of South Eucalyptus Drive", replied Boudreaux.

De Operator axed, "Can you spell dat for me?"

Dere was a long pause and finally Boudreaux said, "How bout eef I drag her over to Oak Street and you pick her up dare?"

86. Gumbo recipe.

We've got our own recipe for gumbo. Get some sausage meat; some rice some roux and a lot of beers. Drink all of de beers. Forget bout de gumbo.

87. Boudreaux sold Thibodeaux a dead horse.

Boudreaux's house had a sign out front dat say "white horse for sale."

Thibodeaux stopped by and offered him $300.00. He tole him he would give him de money now and come back tomorrow wit' a traylor to pick up de horse.

When Thibodeaux came de next day to pick up de horse, he noticed eet was not in de field.

He knocked on de door to de house and Boudreaux

came out. He looked like he had a really bad hangover. Thibodeaux axed for hees horse.

Boudreaux Said, "Tee, de horse is dead, and las night I had too much beer and played too much Bourre and lost all of your money, I can't pay you back."

Thibodeaux said, "Dat's all rat, jus load de horse up on my traylor."

Boudreaux said, "Tee, you don't understand, DA HORSE IS DEAD."

Thibodeaux said, "Jus load em up, I can still use eet for what I wanted em for. I'm going to raffle eet off.

A couple of weeks later, Boudreaux saw Thibodeaux and axed him, "Did you have a lot of people mad at you for buying a raffle ticket on a dead horse.

Thibodeaux said, "Oh nobody was mad, except one, an' I gave em hees money back."

88. Pierre don't want hees whiskey bottle to be broke.

Pierre was staggering home wit' a small whiskey bottle in hees back pocket he slipped and fell. Struggling to hees feet, he felt something wet running down hees leg.

"Please, God," he shouted, "please let eet be blood!"

89. Leblanc drinks beer w'it hees broders.

LeBlanc went into de bar. De bartender asks him, "what can I do for you today?" LeBlanc says. "I'll have tree beers, please."

So de bartender brought him tree beers and LeBlanc started to alternately sip one, den de udder, den de third until dey' were gone. He den order tree more.

De bartender say, "LeBlanc, I know you like dem cold, but you don't have to order tree at a time. I'll keep an eye out and when you get low I'll bring you a fresh cold one."

LeBlanc says, "You don't understand. I have two broders, one in New Orleans and one in Nort Louisiana in Shreveport. We promised each udder dat every Saturday night we'd still drink togeder. So rat now, my broders have tree beers too, and we're drinking togeder.

De bartender taught dat was a wonderful custom. Every week LeBlanc came in and ordered tree beers.

Den one week he came in and ordered only two. He drank dem and den ordered two more.

De bartender said to him, "I know bout what your custom is, and I'd like to say dat I'm sorry dat one of your broders died."

LeBlanc said, "Oh no, my broders are fine----I just quit drinking."

90. Pierre wanted to know is dat is tru 'bout hees house.

Pierre was gonna try to sell hees house. After signing up wit' an real estate agent. De agent wrote up a bunch of sales blurb bout de house dat made everything sound wonderful.

After Pierre read eet, he turned to de agent and axed, "Have I got all you say here?"

De agent said, "Certainly you have...Why do you ask?"

Pierre replied, "cancel de sale...its too good to let eet go at dat price."

91. Boudreaux bot Saint Patrick's scull.

Pierre Boudreaux from, New Orleans; flew to Knock Airport in de west of Ireland on business. As he walked down de stairs from de plane onto de runway he noticed a small Irishman standing beside a long table wit' an assortment of Human Skulls.

"Whatcha doin?" axed Pierre.

"I'm selling skulls", replied the Irishman.

Pierre said, "What kinda skulls do ya have?"

"Well, I have the skulls of the most famous Irishmen that ever lived!" said the Irishman.

"Dats great!" said Pierre. "Gimme some names!"

"Well!" said the Irishman, pointing to various skulls. "That one there is James Joyce, the famous author and playwright, that one there is St. Brendan, the Navigator, that's Michael Collins the leader of the 1916 rising, and that one there is St. Patrick, the Patron Saint of Ireland, God bless his soul."

"Wait a minute", said Pierre "Mais did I heard you say St. Patrick?"

"That's correct", said de Irishman.

"I have to have dat!" said Pierre and paid him £50.00 in cash.

Pierre flew back to New Orleans and mounted hees Skull on de wall in hees bar. People came from all over America to view dis famous Skull.

He made a fortune over a five-year period and retired a very rich man. During hees retirement, he decided to go back to visit Ireland, de Land dat made him a fortune.

Pierre flew back into Knock airport, and while walking down de stairs saw de same Irishman at de bottom of de stairs.

"God", said Pierre, "What are you doing?"

"I'm selling skulls", replied the Irishman.

"And what kinda skulls do you have now?" axed Pierre.

"Well, I have the skulls of the most famous Irishmen that ever lived!" said the Irishman.

"Dat's great!" said Pierre. "Who are dey!"

"Well!" said the Irishman, pointing to various skulls. "That one there is James Joyce, the famous author and playwright, that one there is St. Brendan, the Navigator, that's Michael Collins the leader of the 1916 rising, and that one there is St. Patrick, the Patron Saint of Ireland, God bless his soul."

"Wait a minute" said Pierre, "Mais did you say St. Patrick?"

“That’s correct!” said the Irishman.

"Well!” Pierre said, I was here almos’ 7 years ago and you sold a skull a little bit bigger dan dat one dere, an’ you tole me den dat de skull was St. Patrick.”

"Oh yes!” said the Irishman, "I remember you now! You see... This is St. Patrick when he was a boy!”

92. Boudreaux and Thibodeaux had not seen each other lately.

One day Boudreaux and Thibodeaux met wit’ each udder. Boudreaux said to Thibodeaux, "Have ya seen Pierre lately?”

Tee said, "Well, I have and I haven't.”

Boudreaux axed, "well whatcha mean?

"Tee said, "It's like dis, y'see...I saw a man down de bayou who I taught was Pierre, and he saw a man dat he taught was me. And when we got close to each udder...it was neider of us.”

93. Mrs. Boudreaux talks to de lawyer about a divorce.

“Well, Mrs. Boudreaux, so you want a divorce?”

De lawyer questioned his client. “Tell me bout eet. Do you have a grudge?”

“Oh, no,” replied Mrs. Boudreaux. “We only have a carport.”

De solicitor tried again. "Well, then does de man beat you up?"

"No, no", said Mrs. Boudreaux, looking puzzled. "I'm always da firs' out of bed."

Still hopeful, de lawyer tried once again. "Well, does he go in for unnatural connubial practices?"

"Sure now, he plays de guitar, but I don't t'ink he knows anything bout de connubial."

Now desperate, de lawyer pushed on. "What I'm trying to find out are what grounds you have."

"Bless you, sir. We live in a small house – we don't even have a window box, much less grounds."

"Mrs. Boudreaux," de lawyer said in considerable exasperation, "you need a reason dat de court can consider. What is de reason for you seeking dis divorce?"

"Oh, well now," said Mrs. Boudreaux. "Eet's because he can't hold an intelligent conversation."

94. Placide gets even w'it Basil.

Placide was pullin' up hees boat at de boat launch when he see Cyril come out de swamp in hees pirogue. When Cyril got real close to de dock, Placide see dat Cyril got a box strapped to de middle of hees chest.

Mais, jamais! (But never!) "Cyril, what you got in dat box you got what's strapped to you chest?"

Cyril got out de pirogue an' tell Placide, "Dynomite!"

Placide he say, "Non, you out you mind, you?"

Cyril say, "Mais, non, Placide. You know Basil?"

Placide say, "Yeah, I know Basil, I used to hunt wit' him."

Cyril tell Placide, "Well, every time I brought mahself to town, Basil, him, he slap me rat in de chest so hard he like to broke mah dam' ribs!"

Now ah'm tired of dat de next time he do dat to me, ah'm gone blow hees dam' han' off!"

95. Marie went to New York to become a dancer.

As soon as Marie had finished convent school in New Orleans, she shook de Louisiana dust off her shoes and made her way to New York where before long, she became a successful performer in show business.

She returned to her New Orleans for a visit.

Saturday night she went to confession in de church, which she had always attended as a child. In de confessional Fader Alfonse recognized her and began asking her bout her work.

She explained dat she was an acrobatic dancer. He said, "What does dat mean?" She said she would be happy to show him de kind of thing she did on stage.

She stepped out of de confessional and wit'in sight of Fader Alfonse, she went into a series of cartwheels, leaping splits, han'springs and backflips.

Kneeling near de confessional, waiting deir turn, were two middle-aged ladies. Dey witnessed Marie's acrobatics wit' wide eyes.

One said to de udder, "Will you just look at de penance Fader Alfonse is givin' out tonight, and I don't have my bloomers on!"

96. A Cajun Toast

Let's hope you are in heaven turdy minutes before de devil knows you are dead.

97. Thibodeaux guides de plan by sticking his han' outside de window.

Boudreaux and Thibodeaux were piloting a plane from Lafayette to New Orleans.

Five minutes in de air over de Atchafalaya swamp, de air was getting rough and da planes instruments quit working.

Panicking, Boudreaux, de pilot turns to hees co-pilot and says. "Jazus Tee...Well have to turn back...none of de equipment is working!"

Thibodeaux says to Boudreaux, "No problem...I can tell where we are by sticking my han' out de window!"

"OK!" say Boudreaux, "Den where are we?"

Thibodeaux winds down de window and sticks hees han' out and says; "Well Boo, we are over de Whiskey Bay. De humidity seems to be gone out of de air. Dat is caused by de water. Jus head east."

Boudreaux said, "Now dat's real good!" and preceded north bound.

Fifteen minutes later Boudreaux asks: "Where are we now Tee?"

Thibodeaux winds down de window and sticks hees han' out and says; " We're over de Mississippi River now. De air is a lot cooler here. Just head in a sout' easterly direction."

Thirty minutes Later Boudreaux axed: "Where are we now Tee?"

Thibodeaux winds down de window and sticks hees han' out and says; "Were over New Orleans, Quick...bank left here and you should be on course for runway one."

Boudreaux, Responds and five minutes later de plane lands safely on runway one.

Boudreaux turns to Thibodeaux and says, "Dat was fan-tastic ...But...Tell Me how did you know we were over New Orleans."

"Well!" Thibodeaux said, " ...When I pulled my han' back in.. My watch was gone!"

98. Thibodeaux waits patiently for the cop to allow him to cross de street.

When Thibodeaux was visiting in New Orleans He patiently waited and watched de traffic cop on a busy street crossing.

De cop stopped de flow of traffic and shouted, "Okay pedestrians." Den he'd allow de traffic to pass. He'd done dis several times, and Thibodeaux still stood on de sidewalk.

After de cop had shouted "Pedestrians" for de tenth time, Thibodeaux went over to him and said, "Isn't eet bout time you let de Catholics across?"

99. Boudreaux talks to a Texas guide while on vacation.

Boudreaux won de Louisiana lottery $10,000,000.00 and went on a long vacation all over de country.

He went on a bus tour and traveled for hours and hours through desert country and oil fields of Texas.

Boudreaux said, "Where are we now?"

De guide said, "We're in de great state of Texas."

"It's a big place," said Boudreaux.

De guide said, "It's so big, dat your St Landry Parish in Louisiana would fit into de smallest corner of eet."

Boudreaux said, "Oh yes, and wouldn't eet do wonders for Texas!"

100. Boudreaux's work crew sings on de job.

Boudreaux got a job wit' de Baton Rouge City Parish Street Department working on wit' a street repair crew.

On hees first day on de job, de crew went down in a hole singing Happy Birthday around de foreman.

Boudreaux axed, "Is eet de foreman's birthday?"

"No, Boudreaux. eet's de third anniversary of de hole."

101. A horse tells Boudreaux w'ats wrong w'it hees car.

Boudreaux was driving along in Evangeline parish, when de motor in hees car stopped. He got out to see if he could find de trouble.

A voice behind him said, "De trouble is dat de carburetor is flooded." He turned and de only thing he could see was an old horse.

De horse again said, "It's de carburetor dat's not working."

Boudreaux nearly died wit' frat, and ran into de nearest bar, ordered a tall beer, and tole Guidroz, de bartender, what de horse said to him.

Guidoz said, "Don't you pay any attention to him, he don't know nothing bout cars anyway."

102. Alphonse can't abide by de judges order.

De Judge gave Alphonse a lecture on de evils of drink. But in view of de fact dat dis was de first time he had ever been drunk and incapable, de case was dismissed wit' payment of twenty dollars court cost.

"Now don't let me ever see your face again," said de Judge sternly.

As Alphonse turned to go, he said, "I'm afraid I can't promise dat, your honor."

De judge said, "And why not?"

"Because I'm de bartender at your regular bar!"

103. Guidry saved de olives.

Guidry went to de bar and ordered martini after martini. Each time he took de olives and put dem in a jar. When de jar was full and all de drinks finished, Guidry started to leave.

"S'cuse me," said a customer at de udder end of de bar. He was puzzled over what Guidry had done. "What was dat all bout?"

"Nutin," said de Guidry, "my wife jus sent me out for a jar of olives."

104. Boudreaux learns from a worm about drinking beer.

Boudreaux was in de barroom every day drinking beer.

Thibodeaux wanted to taught Boudreaux a lesson, so he tole de bartender to give him a glass of water and a glass of beer.

Thibodeaux went outside and found two worms.

He put one in de water and eet wiggled around, he put de udder one in de beer and eet curled up and died.

Thibodeaux axed Boudreaux, "What did you learn?"

Boudreaux said, "Eef I keep drinking beer I won't get worms."

105. The twins are at it again.

Two men were in de barroom and drinking lots of beer.

One said to de udder, "where are you from."

He answered, "I'm from Louisiana."

"You don't say, what a coincidence," de first one said. "I'm from Louisiana too."

Where in Louisiana are you from?

De udder answered, "Breaux Bridge."

De first one said, "I can't believe dat, I'm from Breaux Bridge too.

Den where did you go to school?

De udder one answer Saint Mary's.

He den said, "When did you graduate?"

De udder one said, "1972."

"Dis is unbelievable!" de first man says. "I went to Saint Mary's and I graduated in '72, too!"

Bout dat time one of de regulars comes in and sits down at de bar.

"What's been going on?" He asks de bartender.

"Nuttin much," replied de bartender. "De LeBlanc twins are in here tonight an' dey are drunk again."

106. De police Sargent axed Boudreaux what hees wife say before she died.

Boudreaux's wife was killed in an accident. When de police questioned him, de Sargent axed, "Did she say anything before she died?"

Boudreaux said, "She spoke wit'out interruption for bout forty years."

107. Ivy tells her papa w'ats in her boyfrien's heart.

Young Michel Boudreaux was courting Ivy Chariot. Dey sat in Ivy's living room, night after night.

One night, Ivy's papa, he jus' couldn't take any more. Standing at de top of de stairs, he yelled down, "W'at's dat young man doin' here all hours of de night?"

"Why, Papa," said Ivy, "Michel was just telling me everyt'ing dats in hees heart!"

"Well, next time, " roared her papa, "jus' let heem tell you w'at's in hees head, and eet won't take half as long!"

108. Pierre an' Charest see de clergy go in an' out de house.

Pierre an' Charest were working on de street in front of a well-known house of ill repute in New Orleans.

A Jewish Rabbi was walking down de street, he looked to de left, looked to rat, and ducked into de house.

Pierre paused a bit from swinging hees pick and said, "Charest ...will you look at Dat! A man of de cloth, and hees going into a place like Dat in broad daylight!"

A little later, a Baptist minister came down de Street, he looked to de left, looked to de rat, and hurried into de house.

Charest laid down hees shovel turned to Pierre and said "Pierre! Did yo see dat? A man of de Church, and he's giving dat place hees attention!"

Just den, a Catholic Priest came down de street, looked to de left, looked to de rat, and slipped into de bawdy house.

Pierre and Charest straightened up, removed deir hats, and Charest said "Mas, and dere must be somebody really sick in dere."

109. Marie pulled a trick on Boudreaux to scare heemself from drinking.

Pierre Boudreaux came home drunk almost every night arount ten.

Hees wife, Marie, was not happy at all bout hees drunkenness.

So one night she hid in de cemetery wit' de idea of scaring de devil out of him as he walked home dat night.

She jomped from behind a tombstone in a red devil costume screaming, "Pierre Joseph Boudreaux, eef ya' don't give up drinking, I'll take you to hell wit' me."

Pierre, undaunted, staggered back and demanded, "Who de heck ARE you?"

Marie replied, "I'm de divil ya' old fool."

Boudreaux remarked, "I sure am glad to meet you sir, I'm married to your sister."

110. Pierre drank de whiskey after de car wreck.

Pierre and Tee got into a car accident. Dey both got out of deir cars and stumble over to de side of de road. Pierre says, "Oh char! What a wreck!"

Tee asks him, "Are you all rat, Pierre?"

Pierre responds, "Just a little shook up."

Tee pulls a little bottle of whiskey from hees coat and says, "Here, drink some of dis eet will calm your nerves."

Pierre takes de bottle and drinks eet down and says, "Well, what are we going to tell de police?"

"Well," Tee says, "I don't know what you will tell dem. But I'll tell dem dat I wasn't de one drinkin'."

111. Boudreaux really didn' like Pyreaux too much.

Boudreaux was walking home one night from de barroom when he spotted and old lamp in de ditch. He picked eet up and rubbed eet so dat he could see better what he had.

All of a sudden a great big genie comes out de old lamp and tells him dat he will grant him tree wishes.

De genie thanked him for hees freedom from de lamp.

Den de genie said, "but whatever I do for you, Pyreaux will get two times as much!"

Now Boudreaux does not like Pyreaux, in fact dey hate each udder, but Boudreaux agrees.

"For my first wish I'd like a mansion full of expensive antiques and beauteeful women."

"Granted, and of course Pyreaux gets two!"

"For my second wish I'd like to have ten millyun dollars." "

Granted, and of course Pyeaux gets twenty millyun dollars."

Now by t'ree time Boudreaux is getting madder by de minute he hated dat Pyreaux was getting two of everything he got.

Suddenly inspiration hits him "For my third wish, I want you to beat me half to death!"

112. Fontenot taught de barber was charging too much for hees haircut.

Gremillion, de barber, was listening to Fontenot, in hees chair, complain bout de price he was charging for haircuts...

"I tell you, Gremillion, de barbers around here have a stranglehold de people. I was in New York last week and you charge me half again what dey charge dere."

Gremillion said, "Dat may be true, Fontenot," "but t'ink of de airfare."

113. Cajun Nicotine Anonymous

Now de Cajuns has a new clinic for dose dat want to stop smoking. eet's called Nicotine Anonymous.

Eef you get de urge to smoke, you call dem and dey send a man over and you get drunk togeder.

114. Guidry was scared of de cat.

Guidry was a complete drunkard.

Fader Clarence met him one day, and gave him a strong lecture bout hees drinking.

He said, "Eef you keep on drinking as you do, you'll start to gradually get smaller and smaller. Eventually you'll turn into a mouse."

Dis frightened de life out of Guidry.

He went home dat night and tole hees wife, Bridget....

"Eef you notice me starting to get smaller and smaller, will you kill dat blasted cat?"

115. My cousin can go as fast as a race horse

My Cousin Boudreaux was in charge of de Racetrack in Lafayette. One day, he spotted a trainer giving something to a horse just before de start of a race.

He went over and said, "You doping dat horse?" De trainer said, "No sir, dis is jus a lump of sugar", put one in hees mouth and said, "Look, I'll take one myself..... see?"

Cousin Boudreaux said, "Sorry, but we have to be careful. I'd like a piece myself." So de trainer gave him a piece of sugar too.

When my cousin left de area, de trainer gave hees jockey hees last minute instructions, "Don't forget de drill. Hold him in 'til de last four furlongs. Don't worry eef anything passes you, eet'll eider be Boudreaux or me!"

116. Boudreaux speaks French.

Boudreaux, do you understand French?

I do eef eet's spoken in English

117. Pierre and Etienne talk about how beuteeful de woods are.

Pierre and Etienne were walking down de road.

Pierre said, "Etienne, can you see dat beuteeful woods over dere?"

Etienne said, "I can't see, dares trees in de way!"

118. Boudreaux t'anks de judge for helping hees x-wife.

Boudreaux was in court for de non-payment of de maintenance to hees ex wife, Marie.

De judge decided to increase hees wife's allowance. So he tole Boudreaux, "I have decided to increase dis allowance and give your wife 200 Dollars a week."

Boudreaux replied "you're a gentleman, your honor, I guess I might even send her a few dollars myself."

119. Boudreaux was shocked when he opened the morning newspaper

Boudreaux opened de morning newspaper and was dumbfounded to read in de obeetuary column dat he had died.

He quickly phoned hees best frien' Thibodeaux. He said, "Did you see de paper? Dey say I died!!"

Thibodeaux replied, "Yes, I saw eet. Where are you callin' from?"

120. Marie didn' know dat Etienne actually suffers at de barroom

Marie followed her husband Etienne to de bar room. She said, "How can you come here, and drink dat awful stuff all night?"

"Now!" Etienne cried, "And you always said I was out enjoying myself."

121. De ole man didn' care 'bout w'at Fader Comeaux was saying.

One Sunday morning De good Fader Comeaux was warning hees parishioners' bout de suddenness of death.

"Before anoder day is ended," he thundered, "somebody in dis parish will die."

Seated in de front row was a leettle old Cajun man who laughed out loud at dis statement.

Very angry, de priest said to de old man, "What's so funny?"

"Well!" de old man said, "I'm not a member of dis parish."

122. Fontenot confesses dat he has been steeling from de lumberyard.

Fontenot worked in de lumberyard for twenty years. All dat time he'd been stealing de wood and selling eet.

Finally hees conscience started to boder him and he went to confession to repent.

He tole de priest, "Fader, eets 15 years since my last confession, and I've been stealing wood from de lumber yard all dose years."

"I understand my son," says de priest. "Can you make a Novena?"

Fontenot said, "Fader, eef you have de plans, I've got de lumber."

123. Fader Alphonse is getting' a group togeder for a trip to heaven.

Fader Alphonse walks into a bar room in Kaplan, and says to de first man he meets, "Do you want to go to heaven?"

De man said, "I do fader." De priest said, "Den stand over dere against de wall."

Den de priest axed de second man; "Do you want to got to heaven?"

"Certainly, fader," was de man's reply. "Den stand over dere against de wall," said de priest.

Den Fader Alphonse walked up to Thibodeaux and said, "Do you want to go to heaven?" Thibodeaux said, "No, I don't fader."

De priest said, "I don't believe dis. You mean to tell me dat when you die you don't want to go to heaven?"

Thibodeaux said, "Oh, when I die, yes. I taught you were getting a group togeder to go rat now."

124. Guidroz liked De Sermon last Sunday.

Last Sunday, Guidroz, a wealthy rice farmer, went to church.

After mass he said to de priest, " Fader, dat was a damned good sermon you gave, damned good!"

"I'm happy you liked eet," said de priest. "But I wish you wouldn't use dose terms when expressing yourself."

"I can't help eet," said Guidroz. "I still t'ink eet was a damned good sermon. In fact, I liked eet so much I put a hundred dollar bill in de collection basket."

"De hell you did!" replied de priest.

125. Mr. Poirrier decided to change his life when he was finally alone in life.

Mr. Poirrier was 77 years old and had worked 80 hours a week all hees life and never had a holiday.

Hees children were all married and hees wife had died.

He decided to enjoy life. He had a face-leeft, got a new expensive toupee, bought ten new suits and a brand new car.

One evening he got all dressed up in a new suit, new tie, put on hees toupee, got into hees new car and drove off towards de big and easy city of New Orleans.

He had only gone a mile when he was killed in an accident.

On arrival in heaven, he walked over to St. Peter and said, "What's going on here? All my life I worked hard, and finally, when I had everything in place to enjoy myself, I was killed.

“Why did you let eet happen?”

St. Peter ducked hees head in embarrassment and said, "Well, to tell you de truth, I deedn' recognize you."

126. De Teacher looking for a moral of the story

In a classroom of third graders, de teacher say to the kids, "Today, class we will be telling stories dat have a moral to dem." She splained w'at a moral to a story was and axed for any volunteers.

Little Michelle raised her han'.

Michelle: "I live on de farm an' we have a chicken dat laided 12 eggs.

We got all excited cause we have 12 more chickens, but only 6 of dem hatched."

Teacher: Dat's a good story, now w'at is de moral?

Michelle: "Don't count you chickens before dey hatch."

Teacher: "Very good Michelle, anyone else?

Etienne: "Yes, teacher, I bot some eggs for my Mama at de store. When I ride ma bicycle home wit' de eggs in the basket, I fell and broke all de eggs."

Teacher: "Dat's a nice story, w'at is de moral?"

Eitenne: "Don't put all yo eggs in one basket."

Teacher: "Very good Eitenne, anyone else?"

Leetle Pierre: "Yes, Teacher, when my Aunt Clotile is in da army and when she was in the gulf war, she parashooted down wit' only a gun, 20 bullets, a knife, an' a six-pack of beer.

On de way down, she drank de six pack. When she landed, she shot 20 Iraquis an' killed ten of dem wit' her knife."

Teacher: "Very interesting, Pierre, w'at is de moral to your story."

Leetle Pierre: "Don't mess wit' Aunt Clotile when she's drunk."

127. Michelle had a frien'ly pig in de house.

A New York writer was on a walking holiday through South Louisiana. He became thirsty so decided to stop at a house and ask for something to drink.

Michelle Boudreaux, de lady of de house, invited him in and served him a bowl of soup.

Dere was a small pig running around de kitchen, running up to de viseetor and giving him a great deal of attention.

De viseetor commented dat he had never seen a pig dis frien'ly.

Michelle replied: "Oh, he's not dat frien'ly. Dat's hees bowl you're using."

128. Thibodeaux brot Marie bad news about Boudreaux.

Marie Boudreaux was at home, as usual, making dinner.

Thibodeaux came to her door. Tee say, "Marie, may I come in? I've got somethin' to tell you."

She say, "Of course you can come in, you're always welcome, Tee. Where's my husband?"

Thibodeaux said, "Dat's what I'm here for, to be tell you, Marie, dere was an accident down at de Dixie Beer brewery."

"Oh, God no!" cried Marie. "Please don't tell me..."

"I have to tell you Marie. Your husband Boudreaux is dead and gone. I'm sorry."

Marie reached a han' out to her side, found de arm of de rocking chair by de fireplace, pulled de chair to her and collapsed into eet. She cried for a while.

Finally she looked up at Thibodeaux "How did eet happen, Tee?"

Thibodeaux said, "Eet was terrible, Marie. He fell into a vat of Dixie beer and drowned."

"Oh my dear Jesus! But you must tell me true, Tee. Did he at least go quickly?"

Tee said, "Well, no Marie...no. As a matter of fact, he got out tree times to pee."

129. Dares a story only a few people know 'bout de Pope.

A few years ago de Pope visited New Orleans.

What most people don't know is dat Boudreaux was hees driver dare.

After de Pope had been in New Orleans for a while he axed Boudreaux eef he could drive de car.

He said dat he wanted to relax some. So dey switched places.

De Pope was in de fron' seat an' Boudreaux went to de back seat.

When de Pope got behind de wheel, he started to speed and weave in and out of cars. De police stopped him.

When de policeman came to de window, he quickly called on hees radio to de headquarter. He say, "I need some help, I jus stopped a very importan' person".

De headquarter responded, "Who is eet?"

He say, "I dono' know, but de Pope is hees chauffeur."

130. Boudreaux wonder why he didn' get de job when he and Thibodeaux bot' made de same grade.

Boudreaux and Thibodeaux applied for de same job at the crawfish processor in Breaux Bridge and dey bot' scored de same on de job test.

Thibodeaux got de job.

Boudreaux axes why did Thibodeaux get de job when dey bot' scored de same on de test.

De boss man said, "Look how you answered question number tree.

Thibodeaux answered, I don't know." "Dat's ok mais, Boudreaux, you answered, I don't know eider."

131. Rene' wanted to bury his dead dog in de people cemetery behind de church.

Rene' Champagne lived for many years wit' only hees dog for a companion. One sad day he found hees dog dead from old age.

He went to hees parish priest and axed eef services could be said for hees dog.

De good fader said "Oh no, we can't have services for a dog here, but deres a new church down de street dat might be willing."

"Fader do you t'ink $50,000 might be enough of a donation?" axed Mr. Champagne.

"Of course, why deedn' you tell me your dog was a Catholic?"

132. Boudreaux shows compassion for a funeral procession.

Thibodeaux and Boudreaux were fishing next to de spillway when a funeral procession drove over de bridge.

Boudreaux jomped up, put hees hat over hees heart, and bowed hees head.

Thibodeaux said, " Boo, I deedn' know you were so respectful for de dead."

Boudreaux said, "Well Tee, I feel eet is only right to show a leettle respect now. I was married to her for over twenty–five years."

133. Boudreaux axed Marie some questions 'bout de box in de attic.

Boudreaux found Marie's hope chest in de attic.

When he opened eet, he found $10,000 in cash and Two eggs.

He axed Marie w'at de two egg was for. She answered, "Oh dats cause, in our fifty years of marriage, every time I was unfaitful, I put an egg in de box."

Boudreaux tole her, "Well for you to be unfaitful only two times in fifty years, I forgive you, dat's ok."

Boudreaux den say to Marie, "Den where didya get de $10,000?"

She replied, "Everytime I got a dozen eggs, I sold dem."

134. Boudreaux gets his life's dream, to see de Pope.

All of hees life Boudreaux wanted to see de Pope in Rome, but he could never afford de trip.

After many years of saving hees money, he called de bishop to see eef he could arrange a visit to Rome. He was now ready to go to Rome and hav' an' audience wit' de Pope.

After bout a month de bishop called Boudreaux and tole him de trip was arranged and eet would cost him $10,000.

Boudreaux got to Rome and went to de Pope's residence. He had to wait cause dare was a real long line of people waiting to see de Pope.

Dey only let 'bout fifteen people in at a time to have an audience wit' de Pope.

When eet was Boudreaux's turn he went in wit' fourteen udder people. De Pope went to each one, shook dey han' and blessed dem. He did dis to everyone, except for de last man in line.

De man was dressed in rags. Everyone else was dressed in dare best clodes. De Pope hugged him, kissed him, and said something in hees ear.

Boudreaux was shocked dat de Pope gave de ragged man so much attention. Later, when he saw de ragged man outside. He gave de man $100 for hees clodes.

He den got back in line to see de Pope again. Just like before. Dey let in fifteen people at a time. When Boudreaux was inside, de Pope shook everyone's han', and blessed dem.

When de Pope got to Boudreaux, he hugged him and said in hees ear, "I taught I tole you I don't want so see you in here anymore dressed like dat."

135. De Sobriety test are getting real tough des days.

Boudreaux was da-designated driver one night. He saw a state trooper pull a drunk over to de side of de road. He said, "Let's stop and see what's going on," an' pulled off jus' a ways down de road.

De trooper spotted swords in de trunk of de drunk's car.

He axed what was dey for.

De drunk tole de trooper dat he was a sword swollower at de circus and demonstrated by swollowering de sword.

De trooper den found some torches.

He axed de drunk why he had de torches in hees car.

De drunk tole him dat he was a professional fire-eater in de circus and proceeded to demonstrate by lighting de torches and eating de fire.

Boudreaux said, "man deese sobriety test are really starting to get tough."

136. Boudreaux taught de Aggie was going to play a trick on heem.

Boudreaux and Thibodeaux were out on a camping trip an' dey decided to go out looking after dark.

Dey came across a deep and narrow river an' dey had no idea how to get across.

On the other side were two Texas Aggies, dey also wanted to cross de river.

Boudreaux called over to the Aggie, "Cher, we want cross to da otter side, but don' know what to do no. You got any ideas?"

The Aggie thought for a moment and replied, "I'll shine my flashlight over this here river and you all can walk across the beam of light."

Boudreaux thought carefully, looked at Thibodeaux, and thought some more.

Finally he called back to the Aggie, "I don' t'ink so. Ah'm not dat stupid!

We gonna start walkin' cross dat beam of light and when we get to da middle, you gonna turn da light off!"

137. Li'l Pierre was scared of de alligator.

Li'l Pierre's mamma sent heem to da bayou for some water.

When he leaned off da dock to geet eet, a big gator came up and snatched da bucket rat outta hees han."

Pierre run back to da house and say, Mamma, I deedn' got no water! A big gator snatched dat bucket rat outta my man'!"

Mamma say, " Son you know we got to has some water to cook weet', to wash weet' an' to drunk. Now took another bucket and gone back down dere. Dat gator was probably as scared of you as you was of eet."

"Mamma", Pierre say, "Eef dat gator was as scared of me as I was of eet, dat water ain't feet to use, no."

138. Boudreaux let de contractor build heem a big house.

Boudreaux won the Louisiana Lottery. He always wanted to build a big house and go on a trip around the world.

He hired a contractor an' tole him dat he wanted him to build a big house wit" big columns on de front. He also wanted de contractor to use only de bes' material and he wanted hím to be sure and put halo statues all round de house.

Boudreaux left the contractor and went on a trip round de worl' for six mont's.

When he got back, his new house was ready. Da contractor showed him de big columns on de front of da house. He showed him all of the quality material he used building de house. He showed him everything he axed for.

Boudreaux say, "Dat's good but where are my halo statues?"

De contractor showed him de statues of angles and saints wit' halos located all around de house, especially in the garden.

Boudreaux say, "Ooh no, not dat. I want de little black box wit' de numbers on it, dat you hol' up to your ear. When it goes ring ring and say halo statue."

139. Boudreaux got his social security check comng.

Boudreaux turned 65 years old. He tole his wife Marie dat he was goin' to da Social Security Office and apply for his retirement check.

She tole him dat he would have to have proof of his age and dat he deedn't have any birt' certificate cause he was born and raised on de bayou.

He jus' say, "Dat's no problem."

Boudreaux come back dat afternoon.

He tole Marie dat he was all set up and was goin' to start getting' his check on de firs' of da mont'.

Marie axed, "What proof did you give dem as for your age?"

Boudreaux say, I jus' opened ma shirt and showed dem ma gray hairs on ma chest, an' dats all I needed.

Marie, she say, "Den why didn't you drop your pants and we could have got de disability check too?"

140. Cousin Boudreaux tried to learn to speed read.

Can you believe? While at LSU, cousin Boudreaux, had to buy de cliff notes for de book "Learn How to Speed Read" cause it took him too long to finish eet.

141. Boudreaux and Thibodeaux make a quick trip to Astroworld.

Boudreaux and Thibodeaux planned for a mont' to take a trip to Houston and see Astroworld.

Early one-morning dey started on de trip to Houston and was back by 2:00 o'clock dat afternoon.

LeBlanc axed dem why dey came back so soon. Dere was no way dat dey saw everythin' at Astroworld dat quick.

Boudreaux, He say, "We left early dis mornin' for Houston.

We were goin' to have a good time and spend de hole weekend dare cause we have been planned dis trip for a long time.

Mais when we were almos' dare. We saw a sign dat say Houston left. So we turnaround and come back."

142. Cousin Boudreaux does a Zoology experiment.

Boudreaux was studering Zoology at LSU.

He was doing an experiment on frogs.

He wanted to see how far a frog could jomp under deeferent conditions.

Firs', he put de frog on de floor and said, "Frog jomp!" De frog jomped almos' tirdy foot.

He wrote on his pad dat de frog can jomp almost tirdy foot under normal conditions.

Second, he cut de two front legs off da frog, put it on de floor and said, "Frog jomp!" De frog jomped almost twenty feet.

He wrote on da pad dat de frog can jomp almos' twenty feet wit' its front legs cut off.

For de tird and final test, he cut de frog's back legs off too, put it on de floor and said, "Frog jomp!" De frog did not move.

He wrote on his pad dat de frog cannot jomp at all wit' all de legs cut off.

143. Ole age brings wisdom to Boudreaux.

When Boudreaux was getting old, and a lot wiser, he was riding down da bayou wit' his grandson, Boo Boo.

Dey spotted a frog sitting on a lily pad. When dey got closer de frog said to Boudreaux, "I am really a buteeful princess dat de ole witch changed to a frog.

If you will kiss me, I'll change back and give you anything you want."

Boudreaux reached down, picked up da frog and put it in hees pocket.

Boo Boo said, "Pawpaw you not crazy are you? De frog said it will give you anythin' you want for one kiss."

Boudreaux turned to his grandson and said, "Boo Boo, at my age, I want for nuttin. mais I'd like to have a talking frog."

144. Pierre and Etienne prepare for a camping trip.

Pierre and Etienne were getting ready to go on a camping trip.

Pierre said, "I'm bringin' a gallon of whiskey jus in case of rattlesnake bites. W'at choo bringin?"

Etienne said, "Two rattlesnakes!"

145. Boudreaux explains to de doctor de worlds worse hurt

Boudreaux stuck a splinter under his fingernail. So, he went to the docteur.

The docteur say, mais Boudreaux dat must hurt! I'm gonna have to stick a needle in your finger to deaden it up so I can get dat outta dere.

Boudreaux say, "Doc just go pull it out."

The docteur say, "mais Boudreaux dat gone hurt."

Boudreaux say, "Dat's ok Doc, I done alrady had de two worse pains dere is in the world. Just pull it out."

The docteur say, "mais non Boudreaux you don't onerstand...dat's gonna hurt you real bad."

Boudreaux say, "mais doc, I can take it. I done alrady had de two worst pains in the world. Just go get it out."

The docteur say, "Ok; hole on Boudreaux dis sho nuf gonna hurt."

Boudreaux holds still sweating buckshot. The doc finally gets the splinter out.

The docteur say, "mais Boudreaux I jus' wouldn't believe you could stand dat! I jus' gotta know w'at was de two worst pains in the world, dat could be worst than dat?"

Boudreaux say, "Well doc I was duck huntin' a while back in the swamp when here come some ducks."

"I stoop down in that water to hide when one of them nutria traps got me right in the groin!! Mais. Dat was the second worst pain in the world!!"

The docteur say, "Poo yie Boudreaux dat musta hurt! But what could be worst than dat?"

Boudreaux said, "Mais doc the worst pain was when I

got to the end of that CHAIN!!!!!!"

146. Saint Peter asked Boudreaux one question before he can get into heaven

Poor ole Boudreaux up and died one day. When he arrived at the gates of Heaven, St. Peter greeted him, "Welcome to Heaven, dere Boudreaux!"

Boudreaux exclaimed, "Mai, tank ya, cher!"

St. Peter explained to ole Boudreaux that there was one stipulation before he was allowed through the gates of heaven. He had to pass an enterance exam wit' one question, and he had to get it right.

Boudreaux scratched his head and said, "Mais, ok, cher. What dat be?"

St. Peter says "What is God's first name?"

Boudreaux answers, "Mai, cher, dat be easy, it's Howard."

St. Peter (laughing himself silly) "HOWARD? May I ask you, Boudreaux, how'd you come up with that name?"

Boudreaux, smiling proudly, says "Mai cher, dat be an easy one.

Our Fadda who art in Heavin, HOWARD be dy name."

147. Boudreaux dreamed he had a millyun watermelons.

Boudreaux tole Thibodeaux that he wished he could have a million watermelons, cause he liked dem so much.

Thibodeaux said, "Mais Boo, if you had a millyun watermelons would you share half of dem wit' me?"

Boudreaux he say, "No." Den Thibodeaux say, "Well den Boo, would you share some of dem?"

Boudreaux, he say, "nope."

Den Thibodeaux say, "Den Boo, would you share one wit'me?"

Boudreaux den say, "Thibodeaux, if you are so lazy you can't wish for you own watermelons, I'm not gonna share any wit' you."

148. Thibodeaux tells Boudreaux to apply for the pilot job

Boudreaux and Thibodeaux are out looking for a job. Dey walk by some building with a sign dat says "Pilots Wanted."

Thibodeaux tells Boudreaux: "Mais Boudreaux. You're a pilot, you should go get dat job."

So Boudreaux goes inside and tells the manager dat he is a pilot, with 20 years experience.

The manager immediately hires him.

Boudreaux comes back out and tells Thibodeaux he got the job. Thibodeaux says "Mais, if you can get dat job, den I can too!"

Thibodeaux goes inside and talks to de manager too. Den manager asks him, "So are you a pilot like Boudreaux? I really need more pilots."

Thibodeaux answered, "No, I shovel manure."

The manager replies "I'm sorry, but I really have no need for that."

Thibodeaux, very confused, say "Mais, you just hired Boudreaux?"

The manager responds "Yes, he's a pilot."

Thibodeaux laughs and says "Mais bro, I got you on dis one here; --you see, ole Boudreaux can't pilot (pile it) unless I shovel-it!"

149. Boudreaux and Thibodeaux convince Fontenot to fly dem to the Nort for a elk hunting trip

When Boudreaux and Thibodeaux got Fontenot to fly them into the far north for elk hunting, dey did real good and bagged six big bucks.

Fontenot come back as arranged to pick dem up.

Dey started loading dare gear on the plane, including de six elk.

But ole Fontenot he objected; said he, "The plane can take out only fore of your elk; you will have to leave two behind."

Dang if old Boudreaux and Tibodeaux don't start a big fuss wit' Fontenot. Dey argued dat, "las' year we shoot six elk an' you let us put dem all aboard."

Dey said, "Dis plane is jus' the same as it was las' year."

Against his better judgement, Fontenot agreed to let them put all six elk aboard.

When dey attempted to take off and leave the valley where dey were, da little plane couldn't make it, and dey crashed in the wilderness.

Climbing out of the wreckage, Boudreaux said to Thibodeaux, "Do you know where we are?"

I t'ink so," replied Tibodeaux. "I t'ink dis is 'bout da same place where Fontenot crashed de plane las' year."

150. How can you tell a true Cajun?

A true Cajun is de someone who can pass by a rice field an' tell you zackly how much gravy eet would take to cover eet.

Talk About Cajun Food

What is a book about Cajun culture without at least a couple of recipes?

This isn't a cookbook, but I want to share my thoughts on Cajun food. A lot of people think the recipes they see on TV or in most big time cook books is the way Cajuns eat all of the time.

Yes, the people in Louisiana do enjoy the style of cooking that is promoted to the rest of the world.

The original style of Cajun cooking involved four things.

1. **Game meat or fish** because most Cajuns were economically poor and provided for their families by hunting, trapping, and fishing
2. **A roux** which is made by combining flour and oil or butter. The roux gives the recipe its flavor, consistency and binds everything together.
3. **The trinity**. Very seldom will you ever see a true Cajun recipe without Onions, Bell pepper, and Celery.
4. **Cajun spices**. Everyone has his or her favorite combinations. You can choose from ingredients such as: salt, pepper garlic power, onion power, paprika, chili powder, dried thyme, dried oregano, ground bay leaves cayenne pepper. Today there are a lot of commercial brands available that are very good.

Just about every main Cajun dish is made with rice. You will find rice will be at least used as a side dish.

The Cajun cook can take a plain vegetable casserole, add spices and shrimp. Now you are in heaven.

Recipes

GUMBO

Gumbo is essentially a soup or stew made with a roux. Only the cook's imagination can limit what can be used in a good gumbo. There are vegetable gumbos (i.e. Okra), seafood gumbos (i.e. Shrimp or seafood), meat gumbos, (i.e. chicken, squirrel, sausage) and combination gumbos (chicken and Okra, or chicken and sausage)

My favorite is a simple chicken and sausage gumbo. This one's easy for quick and great evening's meal.

- 1 cup oil
- 1 cup flour
- 1 large onions, chopped
- 2 bell peppers, chopped
- 4 ribs celery, chopped
- 4 - 6 cloves garlic, minced
- 4 quarts chicken stock
- 2 bay leaves
- 2 teaspoons Creole seasoning, (to taste)
- 1 teaspoon dried thyme leaves
- Salt and freshly ground black pepper to taste
- 1 large chicken (young hen preferred), cut into pieces

- 2/3 cup fresh chopped parsley
- 1 bunch scallions (green onions), tops only, chopped
- 2 pounds andouille or smoked sausage, cut into 1/2" pieces

Season the chicken with salt, pepper and Creole seasoning and brown quickly. Brown the sausage; pour off fat and reserve meats.

In a large, heavy pot, heat the oil and cook the flour in the oil over medium to high heat (depending on your roux-making skill), **stirring constantly**, until the roux reaches a dark reddish-brown color, almost the color of coffee or milk chocolate for a Cajun-style roux. If you want to save time, or prefer a more New Orleans-style roux, cook it to a medium, peanut-butter color, over lower heat if you're nervous about burning it.

Add the vegetables and stir quickly. This cooks the vegetables and also stops the roux from cooking further. Continue to cook, stirring constantly, for about 4 minutes. Add the stock, seasonings, chicken and sausage. Bring to a boil, and then cook for about one hour, skimming fat off the top.

Add the chopped scallion tops and parsley, and heat for 5 minutes. Serve over rice in large shallow bowls. Add the file' to taste at the table.

Serve with your favorite beverage and lots of hot, crispy French bread. A simple table salad with a vinegar and oil dressing would complete this meal. YIELD: About 12 entrée sized servings.

Jambalaya

I could eat my weight in good Jambalaya There is no rule on what kind of meat to use. It is up to the cook and their taste or mood. My favòrite is chicken and smoked sausage. This recipe is basic for all different kinds of jambalaya. (Just substitute different meats, seafood or game).

Basic Jambalaya Ingredients

- ❑ 2 pounds meat (shrimp, chicken, sausage, squirrel, pork chops, ham, etc.)
- ❑ 2 tablespoons of flour
- ❑ salt and pepper to taste
- ❑ red pepper to taste
- ❑ 2 tablespoons of shortening
- ❑ 2 cloves of garlic - minced
- ❑ 1 1/2 cup onions, chopped
- ❑ 1/2 cup green peppers, chopped
- ❑ 1/2 cup celery, chopped
- ❑ 2 cup water (you can substitute equal amounts of chicken broth)
- ❑ 1 can whole tomatoes
- ❑ 1 small can tomato paste
- ❑ 2 cups raw rice
- ❑ 1 1/2 cup chopped green onion tops

If you like a little more spice, add a good commercial Cajun spice mixture (too your taste). I like to add Louisiana hot sauce (Cayenne pepper sauce) or Tabasco to mine before eating.

Heat shortening, add flour and let it cook slowly, until the roux is golden brown-while stirring constantly. Add onions, peppers, celery, and garlic.

Cook slowly until transparent, stirring often, then add tomatoes and let cook until oil rises to top. Stir in raw rice, raw meat, and 2 cups of water.

Cook, covered, over low heat until rice is tender. Add more oil and water if mixture appears to be too dry. Add minced parsley and onion tops. Serve hot.

This recipe is great to cook outside with friends and neighbors enjoying themselves together. It can be a full main dish with a salad on the side. Or may be used as a side dish. Always serve with good hot and crispy French bread

Yield: 8 Servings

CRAWFISH ETOUFFEE

- 1 stick butter or margarine
- 2 cups chopped onions
- 1 cup chopped celery
- 1/2 cup chopped green bell peppers
- 1 pound peeled crawfish tails
- 2 teaspoons minced garlic
- 2 bay leaves
- 1 Tablespoon flour
- 1 cup water
- 1 teaspoon salt
- ¼ teaspoon of cayenne pepper (to taste)
- 2 Tablespoons finely chopped parsley
- 3 Tablespoons chopped green onions

In a large sauté pan, over medium high heat, melt the butter. Add the onions, celery, and bell peppers. Sauté until the vegetables are wilted, (about 10 to 12 minutes). Add the crawfish garlic, and bay leaves. Reduce heat to medium. Cook for 10 to 12 minutes, stirring occasionally. Dissolve the flour in the water. Add the mixture. Season with salt and cayenne pepper. Stir until the mixture thickens, about 4 minutes. Stir in the parsley and green onions and continue cooking for 2 minutes. Serve over steamed rice.

Substitute Shrimp or Lobster if Crawfish is not available. I have used chicken. It may surprise you

Red Beans and Rice

This is about the most basic staple recipe of all Cajun food. I am not aware on anyone in South Louisiana (Cajun or not) who doesn't like this dish. Tradition goes that all Louisiana households served Red Beans and Rice every Monday because, that is the day that mama washed the clothes. She would put the beans on the stove and cook them all day while she did the wash.

- 1 pound kidney beans
- 1 pound smoked sausage
- 1 onion - chopped
- 1 bell pepper - chopped
- 2 stalks celery – chopped
- 4 cloves garlic minced
- 1 teaspoon Salt (to taste)
- 2 teaspoons Cajun spice (to taste)
- 2 bay leaves
- 1 Tablespoon baking soda
- 6 cups water

Wash beans and let soak in water and baking soda for at least one hour. This tenderizes the beans and reduces their gas potential. Cut the sausage into bite size pieces. Add all ingredients to the stockpot except beans. Sauté the ingredients until they are wilted. Add beans and cover with water (about one inch above the beans).

Cook on a medium to low heat (don't let the water roll too much) stirring once in a while, for about an hour and a half.

The water level should remain about an inch over the beans until they start go get tender. When the beans are tender, skim excess juice and mash some of the beans on the bottom to thicken juice. Keep extra juice if needed when beans are reheated another time.

Serve over rice. Add Louisiana hot sauce to taste.

No good Cajun meal is complete without dessert.
May I suggest something real good?

Pecan Pie

- 3 eggs
- 1/2 cups sugar
- 1 cup white or dark Karo syrup
- 1 cup chopped pecans
- 1 teaspoon vanilla extract
- 1/2 teaspoon salt

Beat the three eggs slightly, add sugar, syrup, extract, nuts and salt. Beat well after each addition.

Pour into unbaked 9-inch pie shell and bake at 325 degrees for 50 minutes or until brown.

Serve with vanilla ice cream and or good Louisiana style coffee.

If I have tickled your taste buds, there are plenty of very good cook books available with excellent Cajun and Louisiana recipes.

Get one and try to cook Cajun.

It's a real treat.

Its not all hot.

You spice to taste.

Invite your friends and have a real Cajun party.

Don't forget to invite ma cousin Boudreaux.

Laisez le bon temps rouller.

Personal Table of Contents

This is where I fill in my favorite stores

No.	Story	Page

Personal Table of Contents

This is where I fill in my favorite stores

No.	Story	Page

Personal Table of Contents

This is where I fill in my favorite stores

No.	Story	Page

Personal Table of Contents

This is where I fill in my favorite stores

No.	Story	Page

Have your name published as a friend of Boudreaux

Cousin Boudreaux has a lot of friends. They have been sharing stories about him for years in South Louisiana.

The positive reactions I have received from people concerning this book have been unbelievable. If you enjoyed this book and would like to see this sort of Cajun humor continue in a published form, contribute to the next book about Boudreaux and his friends.

I am starting to collect more stories for the next book. If I use your story in the published edition, I will give you credit as the submitter and send you a signed copy of the first edition after printing.

Speaking from experience, this can be an exciting project for you and your family. Your name will be in a published book next to a story that you submitted.

If the same story is submitted by two or more people and I include it in the book, the first story received will be considered. That is a good reason to get your submission in as early as possible.

The story can be original or one that has been passed around. It's language must be family orientated.

Send to: Larry Boudreaux
P.O. Box 87163
Baton Rouge, LA 70879
or
E-mail: Cousin@Boudreuax.com

Order form

1 - Dat Boudreaux Ain't Me, It's Ma Cousin $12.00
This is Larry Boudreaux's first joke book. It contains a dictionary, 150 jokes, and recipes.

2 - Aham Gonna Tell You Again, Dat Boudreaux Ain't Me, It's Ma Cousin $12.00
Larry Boudreaux's second joke book using the same popular format as the first book, but no repeated jokes or recipes.

3 - Boudreaux Cajun Party Guide $12.95
A wonderful book designed to give the party host all the information needed to give the perfect Cajun Party. It contains: kinds of parties, games, music, recipes, sources, and jokes.

4 - Custom Cajun Joke Book *(Stories 'bout Boudreaux and Thibodeaux)* $ 4.95
A 24 page, saddle stitched custom joke. The jokes in this book use two names that the customer chooses instead of Boudreaux and Thibodeaux. Choose your name and your best friend's name.

5 - Over 100 Reasons to Tell You Are From Louisiana Eef ... $ 4.95
A small saddle stitched book, repeats the party warm-up section of this book. This is a perfect company giveaway.

6 - Party Pack $30.00
Includes 3 books: Boudreaux Cajun Party Guide, Dat Boudreaux Ain't Me, It's Ma Cousin, Aham Gonna Tell You Again, Dat Boudreaux Ain't Me, It's Ma Cousin. - $36.95 value

For faster response,
use your credit card,
order on the internet.
www.cousin.boudreaux.com

*** Send Check or Money Order to:**

Boudreaux Cajun General Store,
P.O. Box 87163
Baton Rouge, LA 70879
email cousin@boudreaux.com

Qty	Item No	Description	Price	Extension
___	______	________________	______	________
___	______	________________	______	________
___	______	________________	______	________
___	______	________________	______	________

Shipping and Handling Books $2.00 each (Covers applicable taxes)

Name____

Address: ____________________________________

City, State Zip: ______________________________

Phone: ______________________________________

Whose name would you like these books autographed too?

____

Names to be used in Custom Cajun Joke book:

____

____

Notes

Notes